FOOD COURT
OF THE DAMNED

D.W. HITZ

www.FedowarPress.com

ISBN-13 (Digital): 978-1-956492-70-5
ISBN-13 (Paperback): 978-1-956492-71-2

Edited by Heather Ann Larson
Cover Art by Matt Seff Barnes
Interior Design by D.W. Hitz

Also by D.W. Hitz

Judith's Prophecy (Big Sky Terror Book 1)
Judith's Blood (Big Sky Terror Book 2)
Judith's Fall (Big Sky Terror Book 3)
Gods are Born
Brady: A Novella
Bloodtooth
Our Trip Through Hell
Garrets Lodge
Food Court of the Damned

Stay up to date with D.W. by becoming a member at
patreon.com/dwhitz

One

HOLLY SCRAPED HARDENED BOURBON sauce and dried-up chicken from the serving pan in the back of Zen's Asian Delight's kitchen. It slapped down inside the black trash bag and made her snarl—she couldn't believe people ate that crap. At 8:55 p.m., the mall was all but closed, her register's take had been dropped into the safe, and though there was a chance a hungry shopper might step up to the counter, she was willing to risk it. She had places to be and needed to get the fuck out of there.

It was the night of June 3, 1993, in Golden Palms, Florida, with only one day left before summer vacation officially started, and she could already feel the call of the endless nights with no school. She could feel the buzz of spending day after day goofing off with friends and partying like nothing else mattered—because nothing did over the summer. It was an era of pure freedom, or as close as you could get before leaving home for college, and in less than twenty-four hours, it was about to erupt for the entire country.

She was on the cusp, and her heart was pounding just thinking about it. She knew the real parties didn't kick off until tomorrow night, but her friends were always ready to celebrate early; they had probably already started, and here she was stuck closing up this fake Chinese food hellhole.

She gritted her teeth, dropped the pan into the slop sink, and sprayed a layer of water over the remaining crust to let it soak. From the front case, she grabbed the quarter-full tray of rice and started dumping it into the half-full one. She wasn't supposed to do that where the customers could see—as far as they were concerned, the rice was all cooked the same day, but Joey, the manager, always said, "Fuck 'em, they can't tell the difference," so in the fridge it would go until tomorrow.

She pulled it, the veggies, the egg rolls, and the noodles to the prep table for a covering of plastic wrap, then she stacked them in the walk-in. She wiped off the counter and, like Joey, said, "Fuck it," as she glanced at the stack of dishes in the slop sink. The clock had rolled over to 9:01, and the mall was officially closed until tomorrow. The lunch crew could deal with that mess, and if they didn't like it, they could suck a tit. Same with the trash—she wasn't going to walk those bags all the way down the creepy-ass back hall at night by herself. It was summer, and jobs would be a dime a dozen. If they wanted to fire her over it, let them. It was time to bl aze.

Holly pulled down the front gate and locked it. She grabbed her bag from the office and flipped the empty restaurant the bird as she walked through the back exit into the hallway that ran behind the food court restaurants. That was the part about closing that always freaked her out. The dark flickering lights, the damp fungal air, and the long electrical conduits that ran the length of the corridor were creepy enough, but the shadows in the nooks for piping and maintenance staff were the worst. They were perfect places for someone to hide and jump out at you, the perfect hideout for rapists to catch you off guard as you hurried to your car, distracted.

She took a deep breath and went left. It was the longer path to get out of the back halls, but it would take her toward the anchor stores, where she was forced to park when she got to work that day—or that was her story, anyway. It was a small mall, which meant the parking lot got full too quickly, especially near the food court, and Holly was happy to use t he *I-couldn't-find-a-space* excuse to cover her lateness when she needed to.

There was chatter somewhere behind her, probably the guys at the Beer Battered Pretzel shop who were always hitting on her. They thought they were real service industry Romeos with pickup lines like "Those curls would look beautiful dangling around my waist," and "Come save me with that angel's ass," but they did give her an excuse to exercise her middle finger. She tried telling them she only liked older guys if they had monster schlongs, but they neither stopped trying to get her to come by their store nor whipped them out to prove they were worthy, so she continued to ignore them. Still, there was something unnerving about the voices back there, like they were chanting their own darker version of some Enigma song.

Holly hated Enigma. It seemed like every guy she dated thought it was the perfect thing to play once they got back to their house to chill, like it was a magic key to every girl's panties. Not hers.

She rolled her eyes and kept walking, even after one of the voices started groaning over the others. The echo gave her the chills, and as she walked farther and as it became more reverberation than voice, the tones made her shiver. They crawled along her back like the fingers of a pervy uncle, and she had to walk faster. She got the sensation that the shadows in the nooks and crannies of the hallway weren't just potential hideouts for creeps but that there actually was someone in each one she passed. Those eyes were on her, and hands were waiting to reach out and snatch her up if she didn't get the hell out of the mall quickly.

Her feet moved even faster. She was running. She turned, following the contour of the mall's bowels, and as she reached the set of double doors that marked the passage from the inner corridor into the main mall by the JCPenney entrance, she slammed into the push bar, the door swinging wide. The clunk and squeal echoed and made her cringe, but she kept running through the open mall and out the glass exit doors.

For maybe the first time in her life, she wished she was back at work. She could have been cleaning those dishes right now instead of being freaked out by whatever she felt was behind her.

But it was going to be okay. A wall of tropical humidity encased her, and she glanced back at the exit as she reached the edge of the sidewalk. The door thudded shut, and there was no one there. She could see into the vast open space that stood before the Penney's entrance—there wasn't a soul. She scanned the sidewalk each way and then the parking lot. No one. Just like any other night in this east bumblefuck small town, there was no one for miles.

She had scared the shit out of herself for no reason at all. Holly grinned and let the embarrassment hit her and fade as she spotted her car in the third row on the right.

She imagined herself with Robin, Phil, and Ryan at the beach. Going there for the sunset over the Gulf was a ritual. They showed up and waited for whoever wanted to hang that night; they watched the sun go down, hoping to catch the green flash, and after a while of deciding the plan, whoever was coming headed out. She was pretty sure she had missed the sunset by almost an hour, so she doubted they would still be there, but the likely hangout spot on a night like tonight was Shane's house. She could cruise by there and see if she spotted any familiar cars.

Holly stepped off the curb and felt around inside her bag for her keys. The red VW Fox sat ready to go, almost smiling through its tinted windows after baking in the South Florida sun for so many hours. The key ring jingled as it came loose, a comforting sound. It told her she was out of there, on her way, and nothing else could hold her back.

The door opened, releasing a wave of stored-up stuffy air. She waved it from her face and dropped into the driver's seat, locking the door for good measure. She shook the stick back and forth as had become her habit before starting it to make sure it wasn't in gear, and she turned the key. First thing, blast the AC. Second thing, push in her Eagles tape, *Hotel California*. She didn't love the entire album as much as she craved the actual song at least once a day. As soon as the tape started, she hit rewind—she needed that intro.

Tape deck whirring in reverse, she breathed and waited. The air started blowing colder, and the radio clicked, and hiss came from the speakers.

This was it. She turned up the volume and closed her eyes. She needed this to get over the last few minutes and prepare herself for the night.

Don Felder started his famous intro, and Holly let the chills trickle down her arms. Her fingers prepared themselves and started tapping the steering wheel as Don Henley started the drumbeat.

She sighed. Man, did she need this. She felt her heart engage and her blood flow.

The crappy VW speakers struggled to keep up with the cranked tape deck, but she didn't care. She sang along and opened her eyes. It was time to start the night.

Holly flipped on the headlights and froze at the sight in front of her car. Her fingers gripped, unwilling to budge. Her mouth stopped singing Mr. Henley's lyrics, and her jaw trembled as the music went on without her.

That thing—what was that thing?

She took in a breath to scream, the idea not even registering that she should be putting the vehicle in gear and driving away. Driving over it if she had to.

The sound of her bellow didn't overcome the song or make it out of the car, because less than a second into her scream, a piece of food was climbing up her neck and crawling into her mouth. It was a smell she knew but couldn't place and a taste that could have made her smile at another time—though, strangely, it was flavored with a hint of iron. It filled her lips and crawled down her throat. It filled her belly as her eyes bulged. It swelled in there as Don Felder and Joe Walsh dueled and took her song to that place she waited for every single listen.

She convulsed in her seat as the speakers returned to hiss, but she was sitting still when the door opened and "New Kid in Town" started playing.

Two

A RED VW Fox drove down Orange Tree Trail, but neither Robin, Phil, nor Ryan noticed it from inside Shane's little two-bedroom apartment. In all fairness, though, a bomb could have dropped outside the rundown apartment complex and they wouldn't have realized it through the haze of bong smoke that filled the place.

Robin glanced at her watch. It was almost 10:00, and while summer started tomorrow, it wasn't there yet. She would need to be home in around thirty minutes if she didn't want to start her vacation off grounded. That was when she noticed R.E.M. was playing on Shane's boombox.

"Fuck, this song *again*?" She rolled her eyes and picked up the bong from the table. "I hate this song."

"'Losing My Religion?'" Phil looked over, eyes glowing red. "It's not that bad."

"That's why you can't keep a girlfriend." She picked a pinch of the Mexican dirt weed from her bag and stuffed it into the bowl.

"What's that supposed to mean?" Phil's face was wrinkled in curiosity.

Robin clouded up the inside of the bong and sucked in her hit. Her eyes still closed, she strained to explain. "The guy in the song is a loser. He's afraid and has no confidence. Girls hate that shit."

"This is the '90s," Ryan spoke up. "Girls like when guys are sensitive."

"Yeah?" She set the bong on the table, and Phil picked it up. "So, how many girlfriends do you have?"

"Shut up." Ryan shook his head. "That doesn't mean anything."

Phil took his hit and contemplated. "She might have a point."

"Don't get me wrong," Robin said, "we don't want assholes—well, maybe just a little bit of one—but we don't want a guy sitting in the corner crying because he can't face the world."

"So what's a manly song, then?" Ryan snatched up the bong.

"Don't you get it? It's not about manly, it's about knowing who you are and owning that shit. You hear that song 'Creep?' The guy says he's a weirdo. He knows he's a weirdo, just like the rest of us. Even if he's got feelings, it's more real than that R.E.M. 'I'm a Rockstar' crap."

"Fucking R.E.M.?" Shane stumbled in from the bathroom he had retreated to twenty minutes ago after swallowing three hits of Pappa Smurf acid.

Robin had already started to wonder if she should check on him but hadn't worked up the energy to stand yet.

"I hate R.E.M." He opened the CD player on the boombox, and the music stopped as he dropped in a disc and hit play.

"Thank you." Robin glanced at her watch again, then turned to Phil. "You driving me home?" She knew he would say yes. He was always the driver, so it was pretty much a given. Plus, she knew he had a crush on her. But he just wasn't what she was looking for. She didn't know if anyone in town was.

"Now?"

"Soon. I don't want to be grounded this summer."

Red Hot Chili Peppers started playing. "Parents." Shane chuckled and plopped into the last seat on the couch beside Ryan. "I remember those."

"We can't all drop out and sell drugs." Robin raised her eyebrows.

"Yes, you can. That's the beauty of it." Shane found the bong held nothing but ash and packed it again. He was the local legend in Golden

Palms High who had been busted for pot his sophomore year and just never came back. His parents, so sick of his shit, cosigned on his first apartment just to get him out of the house. When he got kicked out of there for being too loud and having constant parties, he was forced to move into this one, but with enough money from selling weed, acid, and shrooms, he was able to pay a year in advance and didn't need his folks anymore.

Yes, he was a legend. But he was also the cautionary tale since everyone in town knew he was going to be locked up by the time he was twenty-one if he didn't take a break from rotting his brain now and then—which he didn't.

"Where's the party tomorrow, anyway?" Shane asked.

"Which one?" Phil rolled his eyes.

"You don't think you'll get the page?" Ryan asked.

"I guess so." Shane nodded and hit the bong. Of course he would. His beeper was always blowing up on Fridays, and that one was going to be special. He'd spend the entire night driving from party to party, delivering his products, with everyone wondering how he could even see straight to pilot the car with his eyes completely black with dilated pupils.

He blew out and stretched his jaw as wide as it would go. "Just thinking about the plan."

"You're going shrooming tomorrow, aren't you?" Ryan squinted and nodded with approval.

"I need supply, don't I?" It was also legend that Shane could find the best mushrooms in Southwest Florida, and the pastures he picked them from were a highly guarded secret.

"Man, I want to go." Ryan shook his head.

"Dude, I'd have to blindfold you on the drive."

"Worth it."

Shane smiled, then blinked one eye at a time. "We'll see, man. Maybe next week."

"No shit?"

Shane just smiled.

Robin stood. "Okay, fuckers, I gotta go."

Phil patted down his pockets, verified his keys were there, and stood too. "Coming, Ryan?"

"Man, it's only like ten after. What's the hurry?"

"I'm not going to be late—not tonight," Robin insisted.

"Yeah, yeah." Ryan grabbed one last hit before rising. "Next week." He pointed at Shane.

"What's next week?"

"Shrooming!"

"Yeah, yeah. Next week."

Robin walked over and gave Shane a hug. He was a fuckup, and he probably wasn't going to live to reach thirty, but he was always straight up and he was a sweetheart to her and her friends. "See you tomorrow."

"Yeah, babe." He hugged her back.

They filed out of Shane's place, rubbing their eyes in the humid night. They piled into Phil's Camry and took a minute to acclimate themselves before Phil put it in gear. They were halfway to Robin's house before anyone spoke.

"Did anyone hear from Holly today?" Ryan wondered.

"At school," Phil said.

"She had to work. That job takes all her time," Robin said. She puffed her cigarette and flicked the ashes against the top of the cracked window.

Ryan tapped at the back of Robin's seat as the tall pines slid past them. "Yeah, but she's the one that's always got money."

"So you're getting a job too?"

"Maybe. I want to do stuff this summer. I heard Lollapalooza'll be in Orlando in July."

"No way."

"Alice in Chains, Tool, Rage Against the Machine, Primus. Hell yeah."

They all seemed to ponder that for a few minutes, after which they all agreed that affording a weekend in Orlando with music could be worth holding on to a job for part of the summer. Phil was the biggest skeptic that they would each follow through, but when Robin said she was in, he was ready to go for it—if she actually did.

"What do we do then?" Ryan said as they pulled up to Robin's house with five minutes to spare. "Do we all get a job at that Chinese place with Holly?"

Robin laughed. "You think Holly could go a whole shift working with you? You'd come out bloody by your first break."

"We could get jobs at different places in the mall? Then we'd at least all be together."

Phil shook his head. "I'm still not convinced."

"Saturday afternoon," Ryan looked back and forth between them, "we all go down and put in applications."

"Saturday," Robin agreed. She got out of the car, pulled the seat forward, and stepped back. Ryan climbed out and took shotgun. "Until tomorrow, fuckers."

"Night, fucker," Phil shouted a little too loudly, and the other two stared.

When Robin got to the front door, she paused and shook out her shirt. She pulled out the cheap perfume she had picked up at Target for occasions like that and spritzed herself, then dropped some Visine in her eyes. She took a breath, then charged inside.

There were lights on and the TV was going in the living room. She shouted, "I'm home," and started up the stairs.

"Robin?" Mom called from the living room.

Shit. "Yeah." She had only made it halfway up the stairs. "I'm heading up—got some last-minute homework to do."

Mom was in the entryway before Robin could escape any farther. "Homework? Tomorrow's the last day of school."

"Extra credit stuff." She thought that was a good enough lie to get her away from Mom before she smelled pot.

"Oh. You need extra credit? I expect good things when that report card comes if you want to do anything fun this summer."

"Jeez, Mom. I talked to all my teachers. I have all As and Bs."

"You better. I know those friends of yours aren't a good influence."

Not this argument again. She just needed to get out of it. They could argue tomorrow. She thought maybe the idea of a job would turn the conversation around.

"Well, my *bad influence* friends are all getting jobs this summer. Doesn't that show some good character? I was thinking of doing it too."

"Huh." Mom just looked at her for a minute. "That is good news."

"So, I can go do my homework now?"

"Fine, fine." Mom waved her away and turned to the living room. "I'm going to stop by your new job and visit you, though."

"Mom!" She continued up the stairs.

"My little girl, the working woman."

Robin barely heard her mother as she rounded the corner into her room.

Neither of them understood how bad of an idea Mom was suggesting. They would soon, though.

The Fox rested in Holly's driveway. The front door was cracked open. Holly's parents were asleep since both of them worked as teachers at

Golden Palms Elementary and had early mornings for the last day of school.

Holly stood in her parents' bedroom doorway, watching Dad snore and Mom face the other way where she couldn't hear it quite so bad. There was an expression of frustration on Holly's face. She knew why she had to wait, but she didn't want to. She wanted to get the next part over with, not wait for the time to be right.

She turned and went to her room. It would be time soon enough.

Three

WHEN MOST PEOPLE IN Golden Palms were waking up and showering, preparing for the day, Shane was driving. After spending the entire night listening to Pink Floyd and watching cartoons, it was time to go to work, and unlike what the residents of Golden Palms thought about Shane, when it was time to go to work, he had a smile across his face.

Pink clouds hung across the sky, and below the crown of tall pines that lined the eastern side of the interstate, the sun broke through with rays that scattered in long streaks across the pavement. He was right on time.

A few more miles north and he would find the exit. A few miles east and he would find his favorite pasture. The image in his mind of those tall, stocky, purple-ringed mushrooms made him giddy. The smaller, brown, umbrella-shaped guys would be perfectly bite-sized. He saw himself at home later with his dehydrator, getting things ready, and he knew it was going to be a beautiful day.

The fact was most people who used Shane's services didn't understand him at all. He had an image of a druggie kingpin, and in some ways, that was correct, but it was only a slice of who he was. Yes, he bought pounds of pot at a time. Yes, he stocked up on pills and kept a book of acid in his freezer. Yes, he went out and spent hours harvesting psychedelic mushrooms, and he sold it all for a tidy profit. But the truth was that he didn't do it for the money. He wasn't a full-blown hippie or anything, but he did it simply to spread joy. He loved the smiles on people's faces when he dropped a sack of ganja in their hands. He loved ear-to-ear smiles when people were tripping balls on his paper or his shrooms. He didn't see himself as a drug dealer; he was a candyman, he was Santa Claus, he was a bringer of joy to all the boys and girls who wanted it. And when schools were out and the parties were getting started, he was going to help make sure his friends had a blast.

Shane took the next exit, passing gas stations and a pair of strip malls. There were a few neighborhoods, and then the fields began. One after another, he went by ranches and orange groves until he saw the proper patch of trees and turned off to find his parking space. It was in the shade behind a thorny bush where passersby wouldn't spot it.

With his shades on, his backpack hanging, and his basket in hand, Shane climbed through barbed wire into the pasture. The scent of cow patties in the thick humidity told him it was going to be a good day for picking. The batch was going to be perfect for the parties tonight, even if there was a nagging in the back of his mind that something bad was coming.

Phil was amazed at how fast the day seemed to fly by. Homeroom was a blur. Most of his classes were filled with either a movie or the teacher telling everyone to chat quietly and sign yearbooks. Before he knew it, the last bell was ringing and Robin and Ryan were meeting him at his parking spot to drive them home.

They passed cars blaring Alice Cooper's "School's Out" and students cheering. Teenagers littered the parking lot with ripped books and torn papers, and the air was electric with excitement. The summer had officially started, and they all felt it like fire in their blood.

They went by Robin's house, then Ryan's, and lastly, Phil's, so they could all change, drop off their book bags, and prepare for the night. They smoked a bowl in the car on the way to the beach, and with the sun approaching the horizon, they pulled up at the 17th Street beach access parking lot, everyone's check-in before the night's festivities.

Five cars were already lined up at the fence between the parking area and the dunes. Freddy Taylor and his two buds waved. Josh Branlin and Carry Weer sat on their hoods, laughing and hiding cans of beer inside brown bags. Molly Star Cozen and her band of hippie chicks stood in the center of everyone, and though most people there were used to it, there were always a few reactions when they lifted their arms and flashed the dark fur underneath. Lastly, as far away from them as Phil was able to park, was Jud Sallas and his angry band of assholes. They were always the loudest, and not in a good way, and Jud and Phil had fought in gym class just after Halloween when Jud said Robin's witch costume looked more like a hobo costume than a bride of Satan. With no clear winner and them both getting out-of-school suspension for a week, they pretty much hated and avoided each other now.

Phil climbed on his trunk, surveying the parking lot. Robin lit a cigarette and leaned against the car. Ryan wandered from one group to the next to gather info on the night's festivities.

Robin puffed as she gazed out at the ocean. The lowering sun reflected in orange rays over the gentle gulf waves. "You hear anything from Holly? I didn't see her at school today."

"Not a thing. I expected her here by sunset—I didn't think she was working today."

"Yeah. Just weird that she didn't make it for the last day, especially with her parents being teachers."

"Yeah, I forgot about that." Phil wasn't as close to Holly as he was to Robin and Ryan; she was more Robin's friend than anyone's. They used to all be tight knit, but it had been different over the past year since Holly came home from some weird summer camp where she was a counselor. Before that, she was pretty cool with them all, but after, she drifted back, only sharing with Robin and keeping the others at a distance. Phil wondered if something had happened that summer but never really had the courage to ask.

Ryan strolled over, smiling after talking to Molly Star. "You guys aren't going to believe this." He paused, waiting for them to react.

"What, dipshit?" Robin frowned. "Speak."

"Molly said Christie Allen is throwing a party." He stood there grinning and waiting for Phil and Robin to get as excited as he was. It was good news party-wise, but that wasn't going to happen.

The good part was that Christie was rich and had a swimming pool. She lived in Sunset Grove, over by the country club, and that meant she could afford to stock the party (and would) with kegs, liquor, and possibly even a real DJ. The bad part was that she was Jud Sallas's cousin, which meant that asshole and every member of his loathsome posse would strut through the place and act like they owned it.

"What else did you hear?" Robin asked.

Ryan rolled his eyes. "I know you guys aren't a fan of the crowd, but it sounds epic."

"Her parties always are," Phil agreed. "Maybe we can stop by. What else did you hear?"

Ryan sighed and shook his head. "There's a get-together at Freddy's place. I think he hates Jud even more than you do, so he's having people over—but it's totally BYOB."

"Sounds good." Robin nodded.

"Really?" Ryan closed his eyes as if settling his rage. "That party's going to be *epic*."

Phil and Robin looked at each other.

"What do you think?" Phil said. "It'll make little Ryan so happy."

"He does seem really excited. Look at his little dimples flaring."

"Fuck you guys." Ryan flashed twin birds.

"We'll go by for a bit, man," Phil agreed, "but I'm not staying there all night."

"You know," Robin said, "Holly hates Christie. I would guarantee she shows up at Freddy's, though."

The wheels spun in Ryan's head for a minute before he spoke. "Yeah, I think we could just check out Christie's place for a little bit. Freddy's is where the cool kids will end up."

With dusky light on her bedroom wall, Holly rose from her bed as she heard Mom and Dad walk in the front door. Finally, it was time.

Keys rattled as they hit the small table by the front door. Murmurs of voices came through the wall, and the front door thudded shut.

Holly walked into the dark hallway outside her room and continued until she could see the living room and Mom and Dad.

They set their satchels by the dining room table, which was covered in piles of graded homework yet to be cleaned up. They passed by photos on the wall from their courtship in a commune in central Florida, where they both had long hair and hardly any clothes on, and they both smiled like the high was just kicking in. It was where Holly was conceived before they both packed up and left for some reason they never explained.

Mom set two glasses on the kitchen island and uncorked a bottle of red wine. Dad stood there watching and waiting.

"It's finally over," she said. "No more brats for three months." She set the cork and the corkscrew on the counter and filled the glasses. She passed one to Dad, and as she took a sip, her eyes found Holly, in the doorway.

She smiled, and Holly approached the counter.

"How was the last day of school, sweetie?" Dad asked. He gulped his wine as he awaited an answer.

Holly took the corkscrew in her hand and fidgeted with it. She looked at Dad and then Mom. She examined their necks.

"You know you left the door open last night?" Mom said. "A thief or a murderer could have walked right in. You have to be better about that."

Holly swung the corkscrew up and into the side of Dad's neck. He was mid-gulp and started choking as he dropped his wine and grabbed the wine opener. He jerked it from his neck and the glass hit the counter, shattering, spilling red wine across the white granite surface.

Mom screamed.

Blood sprayed from Dad's neck.

Holly grabbed a steak knife from the block by the sink and thrust it into her mother just below the jawline.

Mom stopped screaming and gagged, like her husband. And just as he did, she couldn't help but yank the blade from her flesh.

A few seconds later, they both lay on the kitchen floor, and Holly was heading into the garage. She came back with two five-gallon buckets.

There was a lot of heaving, but she finally got Mom and Dad on separate counters, their heads hanging off the edges. She slit their throats wider and let the buckets collect the blood. When she thought they had been drained as much as they could be, she loaded the buckets into her VW and headed to the mall.

Her master would be pleased.

Four

T HE SUNSET PASSED AND the night began, but before Ryan, Phil, and Robin were ready to deal with the complexities of the Golden Palms teen nightlife scene, they needed to refuel. So they stopped for tacos.

Taco Dave's was halfway between the beach and Sunset Grove, where Christie Allen lived. It also happened to be across the street from the mall, which was open until ten on Fridays and Saturdays, so it was only natural that once the food was gone the subject of Holly would come up. From there, they decided to check out Zen's Asian Delight to see if she was, indeed, working and if she was coming out tonight.

When they pulled up to the food court entrance at 9:45, the parking lot was nearly empty. Fridays were sometimes busy at the Golden Palms Mall, but apparently, on the last day of school, people had better stuff to do. Still, they did notice that Holly's red Fox was parked in the first row.

"There," Robin called out and pointed. "She must be working."

"Man, that sucks." Phil parked a few spaces down. "But at least she should be off soon."

"Let's go tell her about the plan," Ryan said from the back. He tried not to seem too eager. It wasn't a secret he hoped one day he could emerge from the friend zone with Holly, but he didn't need to hear the taunts. It was a natural thing as far as he was concerned. She was attractive, and so was he—as far as he saw it. There was no reason he couldn't eventually win her over. In the meantime, she was cool; he really enjoyed just hanging around her, even if nothing more ever blossomed from it.

The tables in the food court were empty except for a few kids down by The Boot, the pizza-slash-Italian place that mostly just sold pizza. All the restaurants were going through their closing routines: emptying trays, cleaning counters, washing dishes. The problem was as they neared Zen's, they didn't see Holly back there.

Phil and Robin took a seat at the tables in front of the place as Ryan went up to the counter and peered into the back. He still didn't see her, but Ryan thought she could be in the office or something.

"Can I help you?" a skinny guy who looked to be in his early thirties asked from behind the register as another guy wiped down their prep area.

"Yeah," Ryan answered. "We were looking for Holly." Examining the guy, Ryan assumed it might be her manager, and he didn't want to get her in trouble. *Better not ask to talk to her.* Instead, he said, "Can you tell her her friends came by after you guys are done closing?"

"She isn't working tonight," the man said. "I think she's scheduled for tomorrow, though."

"Oh." That caught Ryan a bit off guard, especially since she didn't show up at school or the beach and her car was there. "Thanks."

"Yeah." The guy popped open the register and started counting, and Ryan walked back to his friends.

"She's not there."

Phil squinted. "But her car's here?"

"Did she get a job somewhere else?"

"She would have told me," Robin said.

Ryan scanned the place from store to store. He watched the workers and the few customers, and a creepy feeling fell over him. Other than the kids goofing off over by the pizza place, most of the people seemed stuck in a track of mindless motion. It was like they were carrying out their jobs with little thought or emotion, just acting like mindless automatons. He guessed it was just part of working at the same job for a long time—it became nothing but a repetitive act. But it gave him the creeps. He was glad that when he started working it would only be for a few months, just a summer job, and then he would be done.

"We can leave a note on her car?" Phil suggested. "Tell her where we're going?"

"Yeah." Whatever they were going to do, Ryan was ready to do it and get out of there. His skin was feeling slimy just standing in the large, empty seating area. It didn't make sense, but he really wanted to go, Holly or no Holly.

As they got up to leave, a maintenance man was sweeping and picking up trays from the table behind them. He looked like he had been watching them, and the man's eyes lingered on Robin.

Ryan's level of unease instantly shot up to a hundred. "Come on, guys." Ryan led them from the table, but he didn't take his eyes off the custodian. There was something off with that guy, and Ryan's gut warned him to keep his distance. It had creeped them all out but no one mentioned it until they were outside writing the note for Holly.

"Did you see the way he was looking at me?" Robin said as she wrote on the back of a Taco Dave's bag she had found on the floor of Phil's car.

"I think he wants you to bear his children," Phil teased.

"Gross."

"Maybe he's just the right amount of asshole," Ryan said.

"That's sick, Ryan. I'm going to remember that. That guy has to be like fifty." She slid the note under Holly's windshield wiper.

At that moment, all three had the urge to turn back to the food court doors. But there was nothing really there. They could see the first few rows of empty tables through the glass and not much else. There was still a feeling, though. It was like they were being watched from somewhere inside, maybe from the mall itself, as if it was a massive entity and the stores and employees and shoppers were all just moving parts of the whole.

"Let's go, guys," Phil suggested.

The sensations didn't make any sense, but Ryan was sure he was ready to get out of there regardless. He probably just needed to relax. They would get to the parties and have some fun, and then everything would be cool. Especially after Holly got the note and came to find them.

It was summertime, after all. It was time to celebrate, despite who was watching them from inside.

Phil was hardly surprised when they pulled up to Christie Allen's house and found cars filling the driveway and lining the curbs up and down the street's finely manicured lawns. It was indeed epic. They parked about a block away and walked, with Ryan leading the charge.

The noise from Christie's carried all the way up the street, and whether she had brought in a DJ or not, the music traveled. Guns N' Roses' rendition of "Knockin' on Heaven's Door" howled from her wide-open doorway, and Phil rolled his eyes as he imagined what other ballads he was going to have to endure. By the time they hit the door, the beat picked up with Stone Temple Pilots, and cheers echoed from the fully packed house.

A half-dozen kids sat outside the front door, already drunk, while one hunched over a puke puddle six feet into the lawn. Inside, the hallway, the living room, and the kitchen were all practically shoulder-to-shoulder with guests. People screamed both with the music and to each other, and it took all they had for Phil, Robin, and Ryan to reach the back patio together.

The patio was where Christie always had the kegs. It was understood that at some point it was going to get toppled over or worse, and while no one understood how she kept these parties from her parents, it probably helped keep the beer spilled inside to a minimum. Phil thought her parents had to know, even allowed it to some extent. It was part of what made Christie as popular as she was. Meanwhile, she was never seen with a beer in her hand. She was always holding a fruity, red drink whenever you bumped into her.

Stacks of red cups surrounded the beer, and Ryan headed straight for them. He handed the first beer to Robin, the next to Phil, and he kept pouring. Another to Robin and another to Phil.

"What are you doing?" Phil laughed.

"Double fisting," Ryan said. "I don't want to be back in five minutes."

Phil didn't argue. He waited for Ryan to fill two more cups, and they began wandering around Christie's backyard.

Robin ran into Molly Star, and before they had finished their first beers, they were all talking about summer plans. As soon as Robin mentioned Lollapalooza, Molly Star lit up, not because she was into that but because she could talk about her and her friend Karen's plan to follow Phish from Richmond, Virginia, to Miami at the end of July. It was definitely a bigger trip than the three of them had planned, but when she asked Molly Star how they were going to pay for it, she just threw up her arms as if karma was going to lead her.

"We're going to get jobs at the mall for a month," Robin confessed, which drew a scowl from Molly Star. "I know, I know. By how else are we supposed to earn money?"

"Drugs," Molly said. "Take a sheet of acid with you. That'll get you in."

"Maybe to a Phish concert!" Robin laughed.

That was when Phil felt someone grab his shirt from behind and yank him backward. His beer went up and over his shoulders, and his back smacked onto the ground. There he was, hovering over Phil with a shit-eating grin plastered across his face: Jud.

"Fucker!" Phil turned over and rose to his feet, and Jud's hands found Phil's shoulders, pushing Phil into Ryan and the girls. "Get off me!"

Phil spun. He couldn't get his fists into position, but he could get his elbow out, and it cracked Jud in the side of the face. Blood poured from Jud's bottom lip as it split wide, and Jud went tumbling toward the pool.

The entire party stopped and stared at Phil and Jud.

Phil stared back, completely weirded out by being the center of attention.

Jud climbed back to his feet, wobbling as he did. He had obviously had a lot more beer than Phil.

"Fucking loser!" Jud pointed at Phil. His face was flush, and his split lip dripped blood down his chin and onto the pavement. "I'll kill you!" He ran as fast as his drunken legs would take him, hands stretched forward for Phil.

Phil was not a great fighter. He didn't really have lessons or training, not unless you counted a month of karate when he was eight and thought *The Karate Kid* was the coolest film ever. What he did have was a pretty cool head under pressure and a much more sober mindset than Jud. So when Jud came running and screaming at him, he just waited for the last second, stuck out his leg, and stepped to the side.

Jud tripped and ate a mouthful of grass, and the yard full of partygoers burst into laughter.

"Mother—son of a—I'll kill you!" Jud rose, his face covered in dirt and his words slurring as they tripped over themselves.

Phil backed away. He knew the asshole wasn't done yet.

"Get him! Get him!" Jud's junior asshole posse chanted from the crowd. "Come on, Jud!"

Again, Jud was off like a bull.

Phil doubted the same trick would work a second time, but he figured Jud was so drunk it just might; but this time, he went the other way. Jud came within feet, and Phil pivoted.

Jud was expecting it, but he wasn't quite quick enough. He was able to jump over Phil's foot, and he got a hand on Phil's shoulder, but he was going so fast he wasn't able to stop himself when he tried to turn and follow his opponent. The maneuver led Jud into one foot going left and one going right, neither able to keep him upright.

Phil's shoulder slipped from Jud's grip, and Jud went rolling across the concrete pool deck and over the edge.

The party erupted in laughter once again as Jud plunged into the water with a giant splash.

Phil was halfway through a chuckle as well when Robin grabbed his arm and pulled. "Come on!" It didn't take him long to see why. One of Jud's friends was trying to get Jud out of the water, but two more were fighting their way through the partygoers, trying to get around the pool to Phil.

"Yeah," Phil agreed.

One, two, three, Robin, Phil, and Ryan slipped out of the back yard and ran up the side of the house to the street.

"You better run!" someone called after them.

When they reached the road, they looked back. They were clear, and all three laughed so hard their sides hurt.

"Mother! Son of a!" Ryan mocked.

Robin leaned in and kissed Phil on the cheek. "Good job, kid. Now let's get the fuck out of here!"

Phil was speechless. He hadn't been in a fight—if that's what you would call what had just happened—since the last time with Jud, and it felt like a much better outcome.

They raced to the car and jumped inside as Jud climbed from the pool, dripping and plotting revenge. Neither Jud nor Phil would expect how bloody their next meeting would be.

Five

P HIL'S EYES SEEMED PLASTERED shut in the morning. When he finally rubbed the crust loose, he found himself on the floor of Ryan's bedroom with a taste like smoky hair in his mouth. All he could do was groan as he sat up and checked his watch.

It was almost noon, and half the night before was a blur. He remembered Jud trying to pull him into a fight, and then they were at Freddy's for a mix of tequila and weed with a soundtrack somewhere between The Prodigy, Nine Inch Nails, and various tracks from *The Chronic* over and over again. He distinctly remembered hearing "Deez nuts" getting repeated about a thousand times throughout the late hours, mixed with a random sampling of weirdness someone said was called Aphex Twin. Only selected scenes seemed real, like when Shane stopped by for a delivery and they shared a joint in the kitchen before he was back on his route like some psychedelic milkman.

Phil picked up a shoe beside him and tossed it onto Ryan's bed.

Ryan moaned and swatted at the air.

"Get up." Phil's voice was dry and craggy. He cleared his throat.

"What?" Ryan pulled the blanket from his face and covered his eyes with his hand. "What time is it?"

"Time for breakfast. Let's see what's in your kitchen."

"Just go. Mom won't care."

"Fuck you. Come on."

"Uggggg." Ryan pulled himself upright. He stood up shirtless and with a head full of hair that looked how Phil imagined Einstein would have with brown, frizzy curls.

When they got to the kitchen, they found Ryan's parents were out, but his little sister, Ally, was there to judge them with cold, piercing eyes as they ate handfuls of dry cereal and drank soda. Before she left for the living room and the TV, she informed them that they smelled like smoky garbage, and Phil thanked her. With that in mind, they agreed Phil would head home and shower and come back for Ryan. Then they would go together to pick up Robin on the way to the mall. When they called Robin, she agreed in her own groggy tone.

It was around three-thirty when they finally got to the Golden Palms Mall, each of them clean, smelling fresh, and clear-eyed. They were on a mission, and surprisingly to Phil, he actually thought they were going to pull it off. They wished each other luck and set off to find jobs.

It was a little over two hours later when they regrouped with slices of pizza at a table by The Boot.

"Well?" Robin raised her slice of pepperoni. "How did you guys do?"

Ryan smiled. "I think I applied at every place in this mall, and you're looking at the newest employee at Quigly's Subs."

"No shit?" Phil threw up his hands. "Me too! I didn't even see you over there."

"I start tomorrow."

"Me too!"

Ryan held up his hand, and Phil planted a high five with a slap that echoed across the food court.

"Lucky us," Robin said. "I'll be working over at the Jumbo Juice."

"Nice." Ryan offered her his hand for a high five.

She rolled her eyes and smirked.

He lowered his hand and picked up his piece of pie. "This is going to be an epic summer. Just wait."

Phil wanted to be as excited as Ryan. He was happy, and he was trying to be positive, but he had to do it despite the suspicion that someone was watching them. He didn't know what it meant, but he wanted to shed the feeling. It was that feeling you got when you were a kid and the midnight path to the bathroom was filled with shadows. You didn't know which one held the monster, but you were sure it was out there.

They raised their slices and bit and simultaneously spit it back out. They looked at each other and then the pizza place, wondering how anyone could eat that garbage.

Phil caught a chill, picturing the darkened hallway to his childhood bathroom, and he hoped he would spot the monster before it got him.

Benjamin Hawthorne cleared off a table in front of Buffalo Chicken, the disgusting fried chicken restaurant, as he watched the mall's newest employees celebrate their new positions with pizza. The chicken stench made his nose flare, but he dealt with it as he sized them up. They were friends of Holly's; he knew that. They were wildcards because of their ages. He never knew if ones so young would accept the process or rebel, but he had faith in the plan.

They would work out or they would be ground up in the process. That was all there was to it.

After a ride to the park and a smoke during a round of frisbee golf, the three of them agreed it was best to get a good night's sleep and show up well-rested for their first day at their new jobs. They didn't go by the beach for sunset, and they didn't hang out late. To Phil, it was almost like a school night, but he was willing to give it a try.

Phil's mom was ecstatic at the news that her son was employed. It was like she was worried he was turning into some druggie bum or something. He didn't mention the reason for needing money or the trip in July. There was plenty of time to bring that up. For the moment, it was enough just to have her happy about something he was doing—it seemed like he hadn't had that since he quit the tennis team sophomore year. Regardless, if nothing else, it would buy him some space.

Phil's room was a blacklight-lit cave with fuzzy glowing posters and dragon sculptures mixed with old tennis trophies and chess club ribbons. His shelves of model cars were topped with CD cases and piles of cassettes.

His unmade bed seemed to call him as soon as he walked into the room, but he made sure to focus as he set his alarm and flicked on the TV. He drifted in and out, watching MTV until he was out for good and dreaming that he was already hard at work at his new job.

Phil stood behind the counter at Quigly's Subs. Ryan was at his right, and even though she didn't get a job there, Robin was on his left. They all wore white aprons and little white hats. In the seating area ahead, Phil watched crowds pass by and sit and eat. There were dozens of kids from his school and various adults who didn't seem to have any faces. There was a guy behind him screaming, "Get to work!" but he didn't know what he was supposed to be doing.

Then Jud stepped up to the opposite side of the counter, and Phil didn't know whether to be embarrassed for having to take his order or excited to get to manhandle his food.

"Give me a ham and cheese, douchebag," Jud snarled from across the counter.

Phil glanced at Robin. She shrugged. He tried Ryan. No help there either, and as he searched the rest of the restaurant for help, there was no one there.

"Come on, asshole!" Jud pounded on the counter.

Another customer stepped up behind Jud, waiting in line. Then another one. The only thing Phil could think of was just to go ahead and make the sandwich despite his complete lack of training.

He grabbed bread from the left—it opened wide, ready for food. He reached into the bay of meats and froze. He saw nothing that looked like ham. Everything in there looked more like... organs. There was a pan filled with slices of what he thought were intestines, another with slices of liver. One had whole human hearts, and the one beside that held slices of them. It was the most disgusting thing he had ever seen, and he wanted to puke, only he couldn't because he didn't want to get fired.

"Let's go, asshole!"

All Phil could do was say *fuck it* and do what the guy asked. In the absence of tongs, he stuck his hand into the mound of intestines and pulled out three, each about the length of hot dogs, and laid them on the bread.

"That's right." Jud puffed himself up and stepped slightly to the side so he was standing in front of the cheese section. Another three people got in line behind him.

"Guys?" Phil motioned for Ryan and Robin to help, but they just stood there.

"I said ham *and cheese*, idiot! Come on!"

Phil stepped sideways to where the cheeses were supposed to be, but instead of different shades of cheese, what he found were slices of different shades of skin. Pale, tan, brown, and darker. They were fanned out in their pans over puddles of watery blood. The edges of each square were dried out and crusted on one side and bloody on the other.

"Give me the Swiss, shitbird."

Phil had no idea what that was supposed to mean. He took a guess and peeled off two slices of the palest one and covered the intestines. His bloody fingers left streaks across the skin.

"Don't gyp me on the sauce, either." Jud pointed at a translucent bottle beside the skin. It held some kind of red liquid, and Phil was pretty sure it was *not* ketchup.

He grabbed the bottle and squeezed a line over the skin. He felt his insides climb up his throat and wasn't sure he could hold back the vomit again. The liquid was thick, with leaking runny, oily threads. It smelled of iron but also like something herbal, like something he would find out in the woods. There were small flecks of green in it, and Phil just couldn't let himself imagine what it was made of.

He closed the bread and lifted the sandwich by the wrapper, putting it on the counter for Jud.

Four more people got in line.

"I want chips too!" Jud screamed.

Phil turned and grabbed the first bag of chips his hands came across. He threw them at Jud, and Jud caught them in one hand—his other was wrapped around the sandwich, and he was eating it.

Big hunks of intestine hung from his mouth as he masticated more. The red sauce ran down his chin, and his teeth were bright crimson.

Phil couldn't take it anymore. He screamed, "Get the fuck out of here!"

Jud grinned and turned.

The line shifted, and Phil expected the next person to demand something else awful, but they didn't. The entire line walked toward Jud. They surrounded him in all but a window where Phil could watch, and everyone—at least fifteen people—turned toward Phil.

Cold fingers ran over Phil's flesh as their eyes met his. He felt hollow inside as each customer's skin turned bright red, and curved, black horns sprouted from their heads. They raised their arms, and each was grasping something sharp: a hatchet, a dagger, a kitchen knife.

At once, all of their arms came down, slicing Jud into pieces as thin as the layers of skin in the serving dish.

He didn't make a noise. Only the metal slicing through Jud's tissues made a sound, a wet, slippery sound with suction, as they raised their tools and brought them down again.

Phil screamed and backed away from the counter.

Blood and crumbs of Jud flew over the countertop and slapped Phil in the face and chest.

He turned to Robin. She had to know what to do—she was always quick-thinking.

Robin stood with a bottle of the special sauce tipped upside down over her mouth as she sucked its contents down.

He turned to Ryan. He was doing the same.

"What the fuck?" was all Phil could say.

He turned to run to the back of the sub shop, and finally, he saw another person. But it wasn't an employee or even the guy that hired him. It was the mall maintenance man, but he was more than just a man. He was wider, and he was taller. His skin seemed to pulse, and ripples traveled along the lines of his muscles. His eyes were red, and his mouth was inhumanly wide. Weirdest of all, though, was the dark aura around the man that swayed and throbbed as if being pushed and pulled by an invisible wind, and when it blew toward Phil, it was like tendrils of blackness were reaching out for him.

The maintenance man was pointing a bottle of that stuff at Phil. The sauce.

"You'll like it," he said.

Six

WHILE MAKING SHAKES OF juice, ice cream, and yogurt wasn't much more complicated than what Robin expected it to be, the variety on the menu was. She had started at eleven after riding to the mall with Phil and Ryan, and then they headed to their separate jobs. It was funny being able to look across the food court and see them getting trained at the same time as she was. It was funnier that her training mostly consisted of her coworker, Chantal, pointing to the wall where all the recipes were listed and then to the cooler where all the ingredients w ere.

"That's it," her trainer said.

That might have been it as far as steps, but the wall of offerings was staggering. The fruits, the yogurts, the ice creams, the juices. The menu varied from smoothies that were pretty much just plain old milkshakes to Californian health drinks with juices, grasses, and powders that she had never heard of, some she wasn't even sure how to pronounce.

Chantal must have seen her eyes glazing over as she read the recipes. "Don't sweat it. Most people just get the standard strawberry banana smoothie or a milkshake. I don't think I've had to make more than ten of those other concoctions."

That was a relief because there had to be over a hundred.

"Just take the order, read the recipe, and make it."

Robin tried to take some solace in that. "But what if we get a line or a lunch rush or whatever?"

Chantal chuckled. "Yeah, a lunch rush... You've never bought one of these, have you?"

Robin was embarrassed to say no, but she did.

"The biggest line I've ever gotten was four people. You'll be good. Just smile and be happy, and make sure when you hand them their change, make them take it over the tip cup so they notice it and feel bad if they don't drop something in. Oh, and never give out fives—always give ones. You're more likely to have them leave a couple. Otherwise, that cup'll just be jingling with quarters at the end of the day."

Robin nodded. "Got it." She put on a fake smile.

"Almost." Chantal smiled, and it was good. "People can tell a fake smile. You have to make it reach your eyes, even squint a little."

Robin tried again.

"Almost. Try this: laugh and feel how your face changes. Then do that."

She made herself laugh, and she felt it, the tiny pressure around her eyes from her cheeks. Then she tried the fake smile again.

"There you go." Chantal fake smiled back. "That'll get us some tips."

During the next thirty minutes, they had zero customers. Robin learned a million things about Chantal, though. The girl had just finished her first year at the community college; she had been a member of the softball team but wasn't good enough to get a scholarship; she used to be a Girl Scout; she was born in Michigan and moved to Golden Palms when she was four; and a hundred other facts that seemed absolutely meaningless to Robin but she did her best to file away. She was just glad to be paired up with a cheerful talker instead of some pain in the ass.

When they finally did get a customer, Chantal did the talking, but they both did the smiling. Robin made the smoothie with banana, yogurt, strawberries, and some weird red juice that Chantal said they were supposed to put in everything even though it wasn't in the wall recipe. After the customer dropped in a two-dollar tip and walked away, Chantal explained the red juice was some kind of secret ingredient the manager insisted they use.

"I don't put it in my drinks, though." Chantal raised it up for Robin to smell.

Robin took a deep sniff. It had the odor of blood and leaves and was somehow peppery. It was *not* something she would want in her drinks, either.

"Yeah," Robin agreed. "I'll leave that out of mine too."

As noon rolled around and the lines for the other restaurants picked up, she was surprised to see Holly working at Zen's. She had tried calling Holly the previous night and got no answer. Maybe she would walk over there on her break later and say *hi*.

Robin got a funny feeling as she watched Holly lift a bottle that looked exactly like the Jumbo Juice secret ingredient and squirt something red onto a customer's food.

She shook her head. There were a thousand red sauces out there. There was no way it was the same stuff.

She got another odd feeling when she looked over at Phil and Ryan and saw a worker at Quigly's squirting red sauce too.

When Ryan and Phil arrived at eleven, they were greeted by a different manager than the one who hired them. They were each given a red shirt, a white apron, and a little white hat, then seated in the office for a series of videos about keeping the meats away from the vegetables and not cross contaminating the stock. For a job that consisted of slapping meat on bread, they were a lot more serious than Ryan was expecting. Luckily, when they finished and were put on the front lines to start working, the other employees seemed a lot less tight-assed than the video led him to believe.

There was a guy standing in front of the meat, and they told Phil to stand in front of the veggies and just add what the customer asked for. That seemed simple enough, but then they put Ryan on the register, and he about shit himself.

Ryan was not good at math, and he even tried to explain that. The manager told him to just hit the buttons and give the change, and he would be fine. When the manager went back to the office, another guy introduced himself as Brad and said he'd hang out and train him. It helped Ryan not have a heart attack, but he was still freaked out that he was going to screw up the money and get fired. But then he figured he got the job easily enough. He could probably find another one if that happened.

At a quarter to noon, the line started. It was like someone flipped a switch, and all of a sudden, everyone was hungry. Customers ordered food from the first guy, and he put meat and cheese and some red sauce on the bread then passed it to Phil. Phil put on vegetables and wrapped it up, and then Ryan was supposed to ring them up.

When the first customer was standing in front of him and Brad told him what buttons to press, he did it. He got through it. But then another customer came, and Ryan couldn't remember which buttons he had pressed. It was like they all blended into each other, making a tapestry of meaningless shapes, and there were more people behind that one. The guy getting done with Phil was watching, knowing that Ryan was hopeless and he was going to have to wait. Ryan was sure the guy way back at the meats and the lady behind him knew too. He was the bad gear in the machine, and soon, they would all be standing in front of him and screaming at his ineptitude.

"Ryan." It was Brad. He was pointing at a button. "That one."

Sweat streamed down Ryan's face. He tapped the button. He handed the guy a drink and took the money. He gave him the change the register told him to, and he did it all again. And again. Before he knew it, he was in the cycle, and after an hour, he actually thought he knew what he was doing—enough to keep the line moving, anyway.

Ryan took a second to scan the rest of the food court. Holly was working at Zen's, and he smiled. He couldn't believe he hadn't seen her since Thursday at school. It seemed like it was last year after so many changes. But somehow, she didn't quite look like herself. He couldn't exactly place it, but part of it was that she wasn't smiling like she usually was, and her eyes seemed somehow off, even at that distance.

A customer stepped in front of him, and he pressed the keys on the register. It beeped, and he did his thing. He looked back across the mall, but Holly was gone.

After the dream the night before, Phil couldn't help that he was a little worried when he stepped up to the food prep area on his first day. It didn't make sense to be bothered by a dream—dreams weren't real—but he couldn't help it. When the first customer wasn't Jud, and all he was doing was adding veggies and wrapping, he kind of got into it. It wasn't hard. The customers told him what they wanted, he added it and passed it on. By the time one o'clock came around, he was actually smiling as he worked. If that was all he had to do to pay for his trip next month, it would be worth it.

Phil glanced over at Ryan and saw him staring across the sea of tables at Zen's Asian Delight. Of course he was. But when Phil followed Ryan's line of sight, he didn't see Holly. He did find that he could see clear through Zen's to the rear door that opened into the back halls, and it was closing. There was no reason for him to care about that, but still he shivered.

Trent Flood hated coming to the mall.

It was usually so easy, though, to run in and eat at lunchtime, his travel agency being right across the street, and that was the sole reason he came—even on the days like this one when he wasn't really open but had work to catch up on. At least he could have a variety of choices, depending on his mood, from sushi to burgers and whatever else. Lately, though, things seemed worse. By the time he had eaten and was ready to go, he was in a bad mood. The food was okay, but the smells, the lighting, and even the general layout of the place seemed to grate on his nerves. And today, it was even more irritating than usual.

He rose from his table in front of Zen's Asian Delight, leaving his styrofoam container, fork, and the remnants of his bourbon chicken and rice where he sat. There was a bubbling in his gut that wasn't going to wait for him to get back to the office. He wished it would; the throbbing in his head especially didn't want him to walk into the alcove-like hall beside the food court where the bathrooms were. But there he was, heading into the flickering fluorescent lights.

As soon as Trent entered the tiny hall, the murmur and echo of the food court dimmed. His head throbbed even harder, and he wished more than anything for a shot of whiskey and a pair of ibuprofen to dull the pain. What he got was a girl.

She opened the doors at the end of the hallway and flicked her blonde locks around to one side. She looked Trent up and down and smiled in that way that told him exactly what she wanted. She looked young, but when they had that look in their eyes, they couldn't be too young.

She raised her hand and curled her finger in. She was calling him toward those doors, and she couldn't have picked a worse time.

Fuck. He wanted to follow her. She had those perfect young tits, and her jeans were the perfect tightness to show off her ass. He doubted he could do it, though, not until after he took a crap.

His gut rumbled, and he told himself he could. He had done it in worse environments before.

Trent smiled at the girl and walked toward the set of double doors. She grinned brighter and backed into the darker inner hallway, then let out a giggle as the doors slapped shut behind her.

"Hey." Trent picked up the pace and pushed on the door. It opened with a light squeak.

The hallway went left and right from where he stood. It was dim in each direction, with enclaves of darkness and the scents of the food court cuisine, bleach, and mildew. He didn't see the girl.

"Where'd you go?" he called. He stepped into the middle of the hall, and the doors clunked shut. He felt a cold breeze, and his stomach growled with anger. He ran his hand over his abdomen. This was a bad idea, he knew that. But there was another feeling lower than that, a warming feeling that wanted to meet that girl. "Hello?"

"Over here." It was a feminine whisper on his left.

He didn't see her, but it was her. She had to have been hiding in one of those shadowy nooks. He grinned at his next thought. He had never done it in a place like that. He walked deeper into the hallway.

"Here I come." His voice was low and melodic. It was wrong; he felt it in his bones, but he liked the game.

"Keep coming," her voice sang back.

She was ahead but he still couldn't pin down where she was. As he kept going, there was a pool of blackness on each side of the hall. He wanted to be in there with her. He could feel his heart rate rise, and he curled his fingers in and out, anxious to hold her and pull her close.

"Where are you?" he asked from between the shadows. "Are you in here?" He stepped forward into the dark with his hands ready to grip her waist and his lips ready to dive onto hers.

He saw nothing but moved into the blackness until his hands were against the cold concrete wall.

She wasn't there. That was okay, because he knew where she was. He turned, a grin on his lips and his hands as eager as ever to find her.

When he saw her in the middle of the hallway, his smile grew. Her arms were up high, and those tits pushed harder on her little shirt, jutting toward him. It took a second before he saw why she stood like that—why her arms were raised.

There was a flash of the dim hallway light across steel as she brought down a cleaver that was as big as her face. It thunked into his forehead, and all of a sudden, he saw her with double vision, the shiny blade between his eyes. Warm wetness ran down his cheeks. He tried to reach for those glorious tits, but his hands didn't seem to work. They were by his sides, and he was sinking, his back against that cold wall.

She giggled again, and once he was on the floor, she pressed the sole of her foot on his face as she pried the cleaver from his skull.

When the blade tore free with a slurping noise, Trent felt the pain. It was more like a thousand blades in his face than one. He wanted to scream, but nothing worked.

She turned and walked away, and he wanted to grab her and strangle her. *That bitch!* How could she do this to him?

As the hallway turned to nothing but gloom an older man in janitor's overalls stepped into view and leaned over Trent.

Seven

Robin and Chantal sat behind the Jumbo Juice counter, talking about Chantal's last college boyfriend (and his poor performance in the bedroom) as the clock ticked toward five, closing time for everyone in the mall. Robin had gone by Zen's on her break and was told Holly was on break too. She had even wandered the mall looking for Holly with no luck. She also strolled by Quigly's to say *Hi* to Phil and Ryan. She saw the bottle of red sauce sitting on the counter there, and though she couldn't prove it was all the same stuff, she was starting to wonder if every restaurant in the food court had it.

With fifteen minutes left before closing, she spotted Phil and Ryan walking toward Jumbo Juice. They still wore their matching red shirts, but both had ditched their aprons and their little white hats.

"Hi." Chantal gave them her patented smile. She was rising from her bar stool when Robin raised a hand.

"Don't waste a smile on these guys," Robin said. "They're with me. My ride."

"Hey." Phil nodded.

Ryan repeated, "Hey."

"How was the first day?" Robin sipped her strawberry smoothie.

"It was alright." Phil smiled. "Better than I thought it would be."

"They let us go early since it's dead now." Ryan gestured at the empty food court. The roar from the early afternoon had been replaced by the low din of roughly a dozen people spread out across the large space.

Chantal glanced at her watch. "You want to head out since your ride's here? A few minutes won't matter."

"You sure?" Robin sipped her smoothie again. It was actually really good. She didn't know how anyone could ruin the flavor with that red stuff.

"Yeah, go on." Chantal offered a smile that Robin had to wonder whether it was real or not. She decided it was. She liked Chantal.

They split the tips from the tiny cup, and to Robin's surprise, she found she was going home with an extra twenty dollars in cash she hadn't planned on. She grabbed her bag and said goodbye, but before they left the mall, she wanted to check Zen's one last time to see if she could catch Holly.

"Think I can get one of those?" Ryan gestured at the smoothie in Robin's hand as she looked around then hopped up and slid across the counter.

"Sure." She passed him her cup.

"Dude." He shook it. "This is empty."

"Get what you pay for." She smirked and led them to Zen's.

A strange feeling washed over Robin as she looked behind the counter at Zen's. The cause wasn't something she could put her finger on necessarily, other than a general dour and depressing atmosphere. It was like someone had sucked the joy out of the three employees.

"You want some bourbon chicken?" the one behind the counter asked. He had one hand on a styrofoam container and one on a squirt bottle of red sauce.

"No..." She shook her head. "I was just looking for Holly."

"She left," the cashier said. His skin was pale and somewhat waxy.

The cashier's hollow expression made something turn inside Robin. It was the feeling she got when she was eight and had to visit Ohio for her great aunt's funeral. Looking at the dead lady in the casket, she just knew the woman was better off there. She had never met her great aunt, but there was an aura that radiated from the body telling Robin the woman hadn't been nice to a soul in the last fifty years. It was like she had already been dead before she made it to that casket and time had finally caught up to her. That was what she saw in the cashier's face—he was waiting for death. All of the Zen's employees were.

The only thing Robin could say was "Thanks." She backed away, grabbing Phil and Ryan by their shirts. "Let's go," she told them as they moved toward the doors.

She didn't see the custodian watching them from the shallow hallway off to the side.

They were barely out of the parking lot when Robin pulled a joint from between her cigarettes and lit it.

Phil frowned and scanned the roads, looking for cops. "Broad daylight? Tell me first next time, will ya?"

She blew a cloud of smoke against the windshield. Smoke rolled across the glass as it spread, and she held out the joint for him to take. "Sorry."

He gave her a smirk and turned north, then he took it from her hand. "I can't stay mad at you."

"What the fuck was that at Zen's?" She turned so she could see both of them. "They looked like a couple of zombies standing behind the counter."

"I don't know," Ryan said. "They just looked like some tired guys waiting to get off."

Phil coughed and passed the joint low between the seats for Ryan to take. "They looked weird. I saw it. Like they were in a daze."

"Yeah," Robin agreed. "A daze, exactly. And what's up with that red sauce or juice or whatever it is in every restaurant?"

"Red sauce?" Ryan blew a cloud toward the front seat and passed to Robin. "What red sauce?"

"Every store in the food court seems to have a red sauce they put on everything. Even Jumbo Juice. We have one that goes in every smoothie. It smells like dirty blood."

"The sounds gross." Phil turned down Orange Tree Trail.

"I didn't see any red sauce," Ryan said.

"I saw it," Phil said. "They put it on every sub between the meat and the cheese. But I don't know—there's lots of sauces. What's the big deal?"

"Maybe nothing." Robin puffed. "I saw it at Zen's too, though. Every store has a bottle of red sauce that looks exactly alike."

Phil turned into Shane's apartment complex. "I'm gonna smell it tomorrow. I'll tell you if it smells like blood."

"Just don't eat it." Robin snubbed out the roach in the ashtray. "I've got a bad feeling about it."

Ryan and Phil glanced at each other and then at her, concerned.

Robin knocked, and Shane answered his door in nothing but his boxers while rubbing his eyes. He yawned and gestured inward. "My friends." He grinned. "Welcome."

That smile always gave Robin a warm sensation. It was genuine, unlike Chantal's tip smile. There was a sincere, heartfelt happiness coming from him that made Robin feel like she was under the sun and soaking in its life-giving essence. She hugged him as she passed into the nearly black, chilled apartment and sat in the armchair.

"You just woke up, didn't you?" Phil shook his hand as he entered.

"Yes." Shane nodded. "Isn't sleep wonderful?"

"Bastard." Phil sat on the couch.

"Good to see you, Shane." Ryan shook his hand and passed, sitting beside Phil.

Shane stretched into the outside air and looked around before coming back in. Robin pulled the last jay from her cigarettes and lit it as Shane crashed on the couch.

They went around in a circle, repeating their thoughts on the mysterious red sauce and filling Shane in on their first day of work and the weirdness around the food court. He listened diligently and pondered, saying nearly nothing as Robin grew even more convinced the more they talked about the sauce and how it was the same, and how something weird was indeed happening. Ryan grew more firm that she was jumping to conclusions. Phil stood in the middle, staying open to the weirdness of it all and swearing he would smell it tomorrow when they clocked in to see if it really smelled like blood like Robin swore it would.

When the joint was out and all of their positions were out in the open, Shane finally spoke. "It's obviously aliens."

"What?" Ryan laughed.

They all focused on Shane. He was dead serious. "Robin's right that it's the same liquid. What she said about the bourbon chicken place, I believe. It's obviously some sort of mind-control scheme, and the red sauce or juice is the stuff that takes control of your mind. Those guys you mentioned are under its power." He nodded as if congratulating himself on his mindful deduction. "It's only a matter of time before they have the whole town."

"I need some of whatever you're on," Ryan said.

"You're just too close to it, man," Shane insisted. "I can see it clear because I have no investment. You saw it, so you don't want to believe your own eyes. You're locked in a logic spiral, dude. *There must be a rational explanation.*"

"Whatever, man." Ryan shook his head.

Shane opened a mint tin on the side table, took out a pill, and popped it into his mouth. "You'll see, eventually."

"He just doesn't want anything to happen to Holly." Robin smirked.

Ryan huffed. "Whatever."

Robin went to the boombox and scanned through the radio stations, settling on "Linger," which she hummed along with on the way back to her chair.

Shane stood and walked into the tiny kitchen. He pulled a box of cold pizza from the fridge and started the oven. "You guys hungry?"

Robin wasn't sure she wanted reheated pizza, but the look on Shane's face—the want to share and spread happiness—made her say, "Sure."

Chantal sealed the last container of yogurt and wiped down the counter. She went over her closing checklist in her head and scanned the place. It looked pretty good—good enough for when Stan opened up in the morning. He was good at finding things she missed, but he always stopped talking when she batted her eyes and bit her lip.

She carried the trash through the door into the back hallway and double-checked that she had her purse and her keys before she let it shut. She hated taking the trash on the way out, but it was hard to complain. If she added it all up, she knew she only really worked for about an hour out of her entire shift, so taking out the trash was a small ordeal for such a cozy job.

Jumbo Juice was at the very center of the U-shaped food court, by the customer exit, which meant Chantal had to walk past all the restaurants on the right side to get to the maintenance exit and the dumpsters, past the flickering fluorescent lights, through the horror-movie passage—God, she hated it. Luckily, she only had a single bag of trash, but still, it was a long hike in those creepy-ass hallways.

She was passing The Boot when she first heard the sounds. Something was skittering in the dark nooks and crannies of the hallway, and she couldn't help but think it was rats. She had never seen one there, but the sound was convincing.

She wanted to stop right there, drop the trash, and give them what they wanted so she could go on her way. She didn't get paid enough to fight off a gang of rats for a bag of empty yogurt and fruit containers. But when she crossed behind Happy Burger, the noises seemed to stop.

Chantal had two thoughts: (1) maybe they had scurried into a hole because her noise scared them, and (2) what if they were being still to bait her in closer to attack her. Number two was stupid. Rats didn't plan and set traps. She had to have just scared them off somehow.

She passed Suzuki Sushi, and her exit was only another two stores away. She just had to keep her wits about her. In a minute, she would be out in the warm summer sun and she would be free to enjoy her night.

But then, the noises returned.

Shivers ran down her arms. The hallway seemed to dim, and the flickering fluorescent bulbs took longer to relight during their dark flashes. The sound of movement returned behind her, and when she looked back, she saw only shadows. It was in front of her and coming from the patches of blackness every few feet. It was beside her, and though she saw nothing, she knew something was moving on the pipes that lined the walls and on the power conduits that ran a foot below the ceiling.

She was surrounded by whatever it was. They were all around her, and that knowledge made her stomach cramp and her legs turn to Jello. She took another step, but she had to stop. Her knees were numb, and she knew she was going to trip over herself if she kept going.

"Help." It was supposed to be a yell, but it was weak. Her heart was pounding louder than her voice had reached.

The lights flicked off, and she prayed for them to return. The bag of trash slipped from her fingers and clattered on the concrete floor as she bit her lip, waiting for the power, dying for the power to come back.

When the lights returned, she opened her mouth to scream. The fleshy red tendrils of something blood colored reached for her, but it was a different squishy, doughy substance that slithered up her leg and crammed itself into her mouth, gagging her.

Chantal's leg went hot as she pissed herself. Her scream was cut short, and her nose was stuffed full of what smelled like pretzels and blood. She wanted to grab the stuff and pull it away, but the sight of the abomination in front of her froze her to the core. Fear shook her until her legs gave out, and she slapped the urine-soaked concrete. The dough dove deeper. She gagged and convulsed, and with red, slimy tendrils hanging over her, she blacked out.

Eight

*J*UNE, *1976. O*CKAHATCHA, *FL.*

It was the early morning, and already the heat was unbearable in the shade of Tracy's little hut. It would have been hot for anyone, but since her belly began to swell with the new life inside, it seemed things like the heat weighed on her more. She didn't think she was more than four and a half months along, but with no doctors in the little commune and no medical equipment, it was hard to say for sure. It was harder to say if the father was Dan or Benjamin.

With so much acid and so many mushrooms floating through the Passage of Peace camp, the days ran together, one after the other. So did the sex. Dan was her favorite—she loved him—but Benjamin was their prophet, and when he wanted her, it was her duty to comply. The stability of not just the camp but the outcome of the world depended on it. His children were the blessed descendants that would remake the planet, even if no one in the camp was destined to see that future utopia.

"I think we should go," Dan repeated. It was the third time he had brought the idea up in just a few days. He lay on the grimy mat beside her, sweat glistening on his nearly naked body. "Something bad's coming." His trips had been getting progressively darker as well. "I saw it. I saw its haunting red eyes. They were like flames. And the blue blobs around them—man. They were bad news."

She would have asked Sadie what she thought, but she hadn't seen Sadie in the past few days. She wondered about that. How many of the girls she was friends with weren't around anymore? She remembered seeing Sadie at worship the other night. Then there was ceremony, and the covenant, which always tasted too much like blood for her liking, but it made her mind right for the dancing and the sex and the—

An image came to Tracy that she was sure couldn't have been real. There were horns and bones and blood and fire. There was crying from a baby and dancing and sex. And Benjamin with his prophet's crown—he only wore it during ceremonies, and even though she was always tripping when she saw it, there was a sensation it was alive and stretching with convulsing, bloody tendrils. They touched her once when he called her into his hut. They caressed her as Benjamin worked. She swore she saw a different face on him that night like he was wearing the skin of another man over his own, and it was throbbing and squirming from between the layers of skin.

The baby moved. It was small, just the slightest change, something only a mother could feel from the one inside her, and it sent a lightning bolt through Tracy. It sent a wave that made her eyes tear up as the realization hit her of what was growing inside.

Her thoughts on the pregnancy had only been surface level so far—technical. There was a baby inside, but it was small, and it would be forever before it was out in the world and real. It was just a mechanical part of nature: you had sex, it grew, and it came out.

But suddenly it was more.

Now, it wasn't just a thing inside her; it was part of her. That movement told her there was a soul in there, and that soul was connected to hers. It was something magical that had happened, not just the combination of two people's fluids. It was an energy that was inexplicably linked to her essence and would be until the end of time. It was love, a love from her being into its.

The tears came, and she knew Dan was right. She had no proof, but she knew if they stayed and she had the baby there, something very bad would happen to it—to her love—and she couldn't live through that.

"What?" Dan saw the tears and touched her cheek. "I wasn't trying to make you cry."

She rubbed her bare belly. "No. You're right. We need to go."

He leaned over and held her. It didn't matter that the contact made them sweat in the day's growing heat. They grasped each other tightly, and they were quiet. The world outside continued, but inside her hut, they were frozen in a moment in time where only that bond between Dan and Tracy and the one inside her existed.

They stayed like that as others moved and worked and talked in the other huts. They quietly planned to pack their meager things and be ready. When darkness fell, and the bonfire was lit and the blood covenant was passed, they would meet at her hut, and they would run.

Officer Alex Murphy kneeled with his team beside a bush on the edge of the property while they waited for the go-ahead. The sun was setting, and thanks to the info from a mole inside, they knew the cult's festivities would be starting soon. He didn't like the idea of doing the raid at that time of day, but it wasn't his call. He preferred the pre-dawn scenario where all the druggies were passed out or tired and the cuffs went on easily—not going in when they were all awake and possibly high out of their minds. But he had also seen the pictures the mole had snuck out—seen the blood and the carnage these satanic wackos were capable of. Since they had the warrant, they had to get in there before more death was handed out in the name of *enlightenment*.

His radio chirped twice. That was the signal.

Murphy led his team of ten around the bush and onto a game trail that took them into the woods. As they moved under the canopy and the sun set, their blue uniforms darkened to nearly black. Their pockets rattled with ammunition, cuffs, and tear gas, the same as the other four teams that were converging from the distant sides of the property. It made his heart thrum inside his chest with a mixture of excitement and adrenaline. They were going to bust these idiots and save some lives—even if the lives being sacrificed were the idiots themselves. Unfortunately, sometimes that was the job, saving people from themselves.

Murphy heard the cultists ahead and raised a hand for his team to listen, gesturing at his ear and then forward. The wackos were already chanting at their bonfire. He saw glimmers of flame through gaps in the trees. The noise was good because it meant they wouldn't hear him coming. It was bad because it meant the crazies would be all worked up.

It was then that the rush in his veins went cold.

He had been on too many raids, being part of the state's Cult Prevention Task Force. It seemed like another hippie cult was popping up every few weeks. But the feeling he was getting at that moment—he had only had that once before, and it was the worst experience of his life. If his gut was right, he needed to stay on his toes more than ever.

When he reached the edge of the woods he kneeled, and his team kneeled behind him. That was position two, where they would hold and wait for the second signal while the other teams moved into place. From there, he could see the fire. He could see the cultists. He could see just about everything, and as he watched and waited for the call, his stomach shriveled into his back and his bowels shivered inside him.

It was like the mole's pictures, but pictures didn't move. The utter horror was not something that could have been caught on film.

They danced. They chanted. Blood ran over them, and blades swung through the air at the height of their reach. The leader, Benjamin, was in the center of it all, on a platform beside the fire. His headdress—it was alive. It was like something from a nightmare the way tendrils swayed from the headpiece, swayed from the bones that built its structure, and the way blood streamed from those elongated tips and sprayed across the revelers. If anyone had asked Murphy at that moment, he would have said it was definitely alive, no matter how crazy that sounded, and it was in control, not that cult leader-fake messiah or whatever they thought he was.

And that guy—Murphy didn't know at that moment if he was all show or the real thing, but he looked like something demonic, like something buried in Hell and brought to life in the middle of the ritual. The swelling and strangeness of his features, the movement under his skin, the look of more than one face merging and alternating over his skull.

It was a thing of awe and a thing of cosmic disgust.

The crowd screamed strange words at the tops of their lungs. Their faces contorted with smiles too big for their skulls. Blood ran down their skin, and below their flesh, there were ripples that bulged and faded as they moved. The most troubling thing about the cult members, though, was their eyes. They were as red as the blood on their skin. They plumped from their faces with pupils the size of coins, and they each looked as bloodthirsty as their leader.

"Fuck," Jones whispered from Murphy's right.

The entire team was transfixed, and Murphy felt their horror as well. He wanted to turn around and leave at that moment. He was ready to say fuck his job and fuck those people. It was too much. They needed to call the Army or the National Guard to come in and deal with this crap, not just a team of a few dozen cops. But then they brought out the girl.

She couldn't have been older than sixteen. She was naked beyond a headdress of her own, though her crown wasn't alive, just a macabre creation of bone with a small skull that could have belonged to a child on top. She was painted in blood and guided to the center of the platform, where she kneeled and looked out.

Murphy could see right into her eyes—they were blank but seemed to be staring right at him. He saw his own daughter in his mind. She was up there with that madman. She was being displayed in that horrific tableau like some offering to the Devil, and he felt himself tremble.

The leader held up his hand, and the crowd stopped everything. They stood motionless and quiet until he screamed.

They rushed onto the platform, their knives ready and aimed at the girl, and Murphy lost what little control he had been holding onto. He was up and charging, his men behind him, and he couldn't hear his own screaming over the repeated blast of his rifle.

The knives came down, and Murphy cried as he fired.

Today. Golden Palms Mall.

Benjamin sat on a pile of boxes in the center of his storeroom between cleaning supplies, rolling trash cans, and mops and brooms. He chanted as he poured a bucket of blood onto the headdress above him. It soaked into Moholam's bones, and the Fingers of Satan stretched from between the cracks. His eyes flushed with crimson, and his face squirmed as the tendrils stretched past the empty sauce bottles and hovered over another bucket and bled.

He saw the Master smile as he did this. The plan was working. Soon, he would have enough witnesses. Soon, he would have enough power. Soon, he would finish the ritual that should never have been interrupted so many years ago.

It didn't matter that his last flock all died in his defense and that he was the only one to survive. This time, he would not be denied.

Nine

Robin had strange dreams the previous night, stranger than most days. Like the ethereal things they were, the details sat just out of reach, but she remembered the feelings. She remembered the dread and the loss of control that hung over her as things and people she cared about very much were pulled from her grasp. When she finally rolled out of bed around eleven, the sensation was topped with an urge to skip work.

The water ran lukewarm in Robin's sink, not getting quite hot enough. She yawned, waiting to wash her face and wishing she could call in. She didn't want to deal with (the red sauce) the recipes or the fake smiling, though there was more than that. It was like her subconscious was begging her to stay away, like it was just a bad idea. But she needed a job. She needed to pay for the trip, and calling in on your second day was a good way to get fired.

"Ugh," she groaned, and washed, ignoring the temperature. She assured herself things would be fine. She just had to get over it.

Then there was Mom and Dad at the kitchen table. It was breakfast for her and lunch for them. They chatted about how her first day went the day before, and she told them half the truth. She talked about Chantal and the thousand recipes, leaving out the red sauce and the stories about Chantal's boyfriend's failures in the sack. Mom said she was going to come by the shop, and Robin begged her not to. She told Mom it was out of mortal danger—Robin would die of embarrassment. But that wasn't quite true. There was something deeper between the waxy creepiness of the Zen's staff and her overall sense of unease. There was a real danger there unconnected to her emotional well-being that she wanted Mom nowhere near.

Her mother said fine, but Robin didn't trust her. Then Mom gave her a ride to work.

It was 12:55 p.m. when Robin showed up at Jumbo Juice, and while Chantal and Stan were there, it was like they weren't. Gone was Chantal's smile. Stan didn't say anything more than "Hello" unless he was talking to one of the three customers in line. And while they were preparing the customers' orders (plus a squirt of red sauce), the entire atmosphere of the place felt off.

Robin put her bag down on a shelf in the back. She hovered there, watching the silent motions, the filling of cups and processing of shakes and smoothies, and she did not want to be there.

Stan's face was pale and waxy—he looked like the guys over at Zen's, like he should be in a hospital bed, not there serving customers.

Chantal was wearing makeup, but even through it, her expressions were dull and cold.

Robin debated turning and heading out the back door, but when the last customer left, Chantal turned and walked past her, through the exit. She was done for the day Robin had to assume, and like that, she was gone. Without a word or even collecting her tips.

Stan turned to Robin and, with zero sparks of life in his face, said, "You're on register. I'll serve."

"O—okay." It was all Robin could say. The cold sheen across his yellowish eyes was too much to do anything other than try to get that gaze off of her. She went to the register and stood there. He was a statue in front of the array of ingredients. She watched him and the sparsely populated court as businesspeople left for their jobs. Distant echoes of shoes squeaking on polished granite and marble floors sporadically traversed the air.

What the fuck is this? Robin ground her teeth and clenched her fists. She stood there, not facing Stan but watching him with her peripheral vision. She felt cold. She knew this was weird, that it wasn't right. But she had never had a job before, and she wasn't sure what she should do. Did Stan have a boss she could question? Should she just leave? She wasn't sure if he would chase her or just keep standing there like a statue if she did.

So she waited. Phil and Ryan were supposed to work at three; she wanted to talk to them before she did anything drastic. She just had to wait, however excruciating it was.

An hour went by. No talking, no customers, no movement at all, and a girl walked in the Jumbo Juice back door. She wasn't there for more than a few seconds and Stan turned and left.

"What's up with that?" the new arrival said. "Usually Stan checks out my ass when I get here, and he invents a reason to talk so I have to stand here while he stares at my tits."

"I—I don't know." Robin laughed. She didn't know if the laugh was from the girl's tone or the fact that she had practically been standing at attention for an hour and was finally able to relax.

"You're the new girl, right? I'm Nat." She blew a bubble half the size of her face before it popped. "You talk to Chantal? She tell you about the smiling?"

"Yeah. We talked." Robin flashed one of her newly practiced smiles.

"Good. We don't get a lot of customers, so every smile helps." She grabbed her boobs and adjusted them inside her bra until they were at attention, waiting to serve.

"Uh, yeah," was all Robin could manage to say. She felt like she had been dropped into *The Twilight Zone*. First her dreams, then the way Chantal and Stan had been acting, then this. What the hell was next?

As it turned out, Nat wasn't too bad. They chatted for forty-five minutes before someone came for a smoothie. Robin learned that the girl was saving to move to Miami, where she wanted to be a model on South Beach. She loved being in bathing suits, apparently, and Robin held her tongue that she didn't think a five-foot-two girl like Nat was going to have much luck—but what did she know?

When Nat made the smoothie, Robin watched as Nat raised the bottle of red stuff and squirted it in with the rest of the ingredients. She got chills. She needed a break if she was going to last until eight like she had been scheduled—she was just thankful she wasn't scheduled to close.

As soon as the customer left, Robin let her fake smile drop and told Nat she needed a break.

Phil and Ryan took turns with a bottle of Visine and headed into the mall. The walk from Phil's car to the entrance was oppressively hot, and Phil rubbed his neck for a slight reprieve from the scorching sun.

They crossed the court toward the back hall that led to the Quigly's employees' entrance, and Phil glanced at Jumbo Juice. He thought Robin was supposed to be working, but he didn't see her. He did see her mother, though, walking away from the counter with a smoothie in her hand.

The back halls were creepy as always, but they were cool compared to the rest of the mall. It seemed like the air conditioning was running extra hard in those dark pathways.

They walked into Quigly's with a minute to spare and clocked in as fast as they could—Phil didn't want to miss a second of pay.

In the front of the store, there was an eerie calm. It wasn't just a lack of customers; it was like both of the other employees were mannequins. Either that or they had walked into the doors of a wax museum, not the Golden Palms Mall.

"What's up, guys?" Phil stepped into his veggie station where he worked yesterday. Brad stepped back, and Ryan took his place at the register. No one replied to the question.

Phil turned to Ryan. Ryan shrugged.

It wasn't right. Whatever was going on had sucked the life out of those guys. They were like pod people or something. He really didn't want that to happen to him.

That was when he remembered his promise to Robin.

Several minutes went by, each worker standing still. Phil knew he wasn't supposed to touch things in the meat guy's section, but he had to do it. This was too weird.

The meat station guy actually shifted when Phil picked up the bottle of red sauce. He raised his hand, moving to snatch it from Phil, when Phil said, "I love this stuff. I just keep wanting more."

The guy watched as Phil sniffed the tip of the bottle and sneered.

Robin was right. It smelled like bad blood and something herbal, just as she had described. It had to be the same stuff at the juice place, which meant it was probably the same as the stuff at Zen's.

What the hell was going on?

"Ryan?" Phil had to show him, especially since Ryan didn't believe it yesterday. "Smell." He held the sauce toward the register. Ryan was raising his hand to take it when Brad seized the bottle and handed it to the meat-station guy.

"We don't play with the food," Brad snarled and resumed standing behind Ryan.

Ryan shook his head and mouthed, *What the fuck?*

The guy at the meat station picked up a knife. He gripped it by his side, his knuckles turning white. The edge of his index finger was wrapped around the blade, and blood dripped from his knuckles. It patted on the floor.

Phil's insides went cold. He scowled at Ryan, gesturing at the meat guy with his eyes. His heart rumbled inside his chest. Suddenly, he wondered just how deep they were in this mess. He wondered if they should run.

"Shit stain, make me a sandwich." Phil spun to see Jud on the other side of the counter, glaring at him.

Was it a dream? That would have explained it if it was a reoccurring nightmare and he just needed to wake up.

"What kind of sandwich would you like?" Meat Guy said as he took a sandwich roll from the shelf on his left.

Jud's glare didn't leave Phil. "Ham and cheese."

It is a dream. It sure didn't feel like one.

Phil checked with Ryan. Ryan shrugged.

The meat guy's hand dripped blood on the bread. He put ham over his blood stain and squirted a puddle of red sauce on the pink meat before placing cheese on top. He passed it to Phil.

"You—uh—you want veggies?" Phil tried for a professional tone.

"Mayo and lettuce." Jud said it like he was saying, "I'm going to kill you." As Phil squirted the mayo, Jud said, "And you better not spit in there. I'll climb over this counter and shove your face in the meat slicer."

"Hold the spit, got it." He put a pile of shredded lettuce over the sandwich, wondering just how much worse that red stuff was than spit.

He passed the sandwich to Ryan. He could feel the hatred beaming at him.

"Fucking douche," Jud growled, and stepped to the register. As Jud turned, Phil noticed red lines over the yellow in Jud's eyes. Jud didn't usually look like that. His skin was also pale, and sweat ran down his cheek from his sideburns. Something was off with that guy—and more than normal.

Jud sat in the first row of tables. He stared at Phil as he wolfed down his sandwich.

Meat Guy bled on the floor as he flexed his hand.

Brad seemed to creep closer behind Ryan, and Ryan definitely noticed based on the look on his face.

Everything was all wrong. Every bit of it. And the longer it passed, the more Phil knew it was worse than a dream. It was weird, and it was real, and they needed to get the hell out of there before they either turned into drones like those two or Meat Guy decided to use his knife on them.

Jud's yellow eyes drilled into Phil's, and he could not take it anymore.

"I quit." Phil backed away from the counter, grabbing Ryan's arm. "We quit." He pulled Ryan toward the back of the store, and Meat Guy took a step after them.

Brad watched.

They moved slowly, like they were backing away from a bear, and Phil's chest pounded. He pictured Meat Guy charging at them with the knife. He thought Brad was going to move at any second and seize Ryan.

They reached the back door, and Phil tore it open as fast as he could. They scrambled through and slammed it again. Phil held the thing shut as they both breathed heavily.

"What the fuck?" Ryan shouted.

"I don't know, man. But let's get out of here."

They ran through the corridor and burst into the food court. They were hurrying toward the exit when Phil spotted Holly. She was in front of Robin, heading into the back hall by the bathrooms.

"No." He stopped there as the hallway doors shut. He was hot, even in the cold, air-conditioned dining hall. He felt the blood heat up in his arms and hands as a sour taste watered his mouth. What he just saw was bad. It was monumentally bad. They had been trying to track down Holly for days, but the feeling he got right then told him they didn't want anything to do with her.

From the men's room, Jud stepped out, his face pale and his eyes bulging yellow. He turned, then he followed Holly and Robin into the double doors of the back halls.

Ten

"**H**OLLY!" ROBIN FOLLOWED HER friend across the food court, but Holly didn't respond. She didn't turn or slow or give any indication that she even heard her name.

"Holly!" Robin moved faster. She had been trying forever to get ahold of her friend. Finally she had her in her sights and she was going to make it happen. She would not lose Holly again without at least saying *Hi*.

Holly passed the bathrooms and went into the back hallway. Just as the door was about to shut, Robin had her hand on it, pulling it open.

It was dark in the hallway, darker than the one she used at Jumbo Juice, and it smelled funny. It was an organic, earthy odor that reminded her of the red sauce—of blood.

Robin caught a glimpse of Holly as she turned the corner. She called again and followed her around. She heard the sound of the food court door behind her opening and closing, and she ignored it. She rounded the corner and froze.

Holly was there, but it was not Holly. Her skin was pale; it was even apparent in the dim light of the passage. She was waxy and blank as if thinking about something far, far away, but her lips were curled into a smile.

"H-Holly?"

There was a cleaver in Holly's right hand. It hung below her hips, just dangling there as if Holly had no idea it was even in her grip.

"Are—are you okay, Holly?"

There was a silence, then, "Oh, me?" she finally answered. Her voice was high and childlike. It was not hers. It was like someone else was speaking through her.

Holly moved forward, and Robin stepped back, only there was something in her way—or... someone.

Robin turned.

It was Jud. Why was Jud there?

She pulled to the side, thinking she could sidestep around the guy, but he grabbed her wrists.

"Jud, let go!"

He pulled her to him. His lips curled just as Holly's had. His eyes—his eyes were like something from a nightmare, yellow and veined in red. They bulged as they glared at her, and she felt evil radiating from him as he stared inside her. Jud reeled her closer.

She heard Holly's footsteps on the concrete. Holly was moving in with that cleaver.

"Holly! Help me, Holly!"

"Of course," the childlike voice inside Holly giggled. "That's all we want to do is *help*."

Robin tried to turn. She tried pulling her hands from Jud's grip, but he was too strong. She couldn't see her friend, but she knew what was happening. Whatever was inside her friend, talking like that, it was raising the cleaver. It was going to kill her.

"Robin?" Phil stepped into the soft, flickering light.

Over Jud's shoulder, she saw Phil's eyes widen. It may have been her imagination or just her subconscious knowing what was coming, but in the shine of his eyes, she saw that huge cleaver coming down.

"Robin!" Phil darted forward, ramming his shoulder into Jud's ribs.

Jud and Robin tumbled sideways and into the wall, the cleaver sailing past Robin's head and cutting the air with a high-pitched *whoosh*.

Robin's skull banged into the cinder block, and Jud growled and spun around. He charged at Phil. Robin sank, turning her back to the wall as Holly raised the blade again.

Jud slammed Phil against the pipes, his stone-like grip on Phil's shoulders. Phil groaned and pushed back. Jud huffed like an enraged bull, pulled Phil away from the pipes, and slammed him into them again.

"Stop!" Suddenly Ryan was there, and he grabbed Jud.

"Please, no," Robin pleaded as Holly stood over her, the grin on her waxy face growing wider. It was like the struggle made her happy, made it more fun.

"Shhhhhh," was all Holly said.

"Fuck!" Ryan jerked, and Phil pushed.

Jud came backward, his foot catching on Ryan's as they pried him off Phil. He twisted and tripped, his giant red-and yellow-eyes locked on Ryan. He opened his mouth to say something, but before words came, he fell on top of Robin, and Holly's cleaver dug deep into his forehead, left eyeball, and cheek.

There was a gurgling sound in Jud's throat. Blood rushed over his wounds and down his face.

Robin screamed.

Holly giggled as she worked her blade up and down with a sloshing sound, trying to pry it free from Jud's head.

Phil's mouth gaped. Ryan's too.

"Help!" Robin howled. She could barely move with Jud's heavy body on top of her, definitely not enough to dodge if Holly took another swing. "Stop her!"

Phil and Ryan glanced at each other. They didn't speak, but there was some sort of agreement there. They charged at Holly, hands reaching for her arms.

Holly reeled back as the knife slurped and came free from Jud's face. She swung it sideways at Phil, and he barely pulled his hand back quick enough to save his fingers. She swung it at Ryan, and Ryan ducked to his left, but she sliced into his shirt and parted the skin on his right arm.

"Grab her!" Phil screamed.

She lifted the blade high once more, and Phil seized her left arm as Ryan grabbed her right. They pushed so hard, trying to preempt her next swing, that they slammed her into the cinder block, the back of her head colliding into concrete with a *thunk* and a stream of blood wetting the wall.

The blade slipped from Holly's hand, the dull spine hitting Ryan on the head as it toppled down. It clanged on the floor, and Phil and Ryan found themselves pressing their knocked-out friend against the wall while they panted and wondered what to do next.

"Shit!" It sounded like wet meat rolling as Robin shifted Jud's body off of her.

Ryan and Phil loosened their grips, and Holly slid down. Phil kicked the knife, and it skated down the hallway.

"Jesus," Ryan said softly. He looked heartbroken as he gazed away from Holly, then horrified as he saw Jud's gushing face. "What—what do we do? We hurt Holly, and she... She killed Jud."

"She's just passed out," Phil tried to reassure his friend, but he flinched as his eyes fell on the gap in Jud's skull. "We need to get out of here."

Robin climbed to her feet and pointed at Holly. "We have to bring her."

"She tried to kill us," Phil reminded her.

"No shit. She's fully fucking possessed, guys. I saw it in her eyes. We have to help her."

———————

Phil was pretty proud of them. The three together managed to carry Holly down the hall to the maintenance exit, then he, being the least bloody, went for his car and brought it over. With Ryan and Holly in the back—Holly tied up with the aprons they forgot to return—they drove to Shane's. In a matter of roughly thirty minutes, they were inside the security of Shane's apartment without either police or parental involvement. They weren't sure how long it would be before law enforcement found Jud's body and started looking for his killer, but hopefully it would be a while, and hopefully they had covered their tracks enough that they wouldn't be the target.

"You sure, man?" Shane leaned in for the fourth time in the few hours since they had arrived. He looked Holly over with pupils the size of dimes as she sat unconscious and tied to the recliner. "How do you know—like, for sure—that she's possessed?"

"Just wait 'til she wakes up." Robin hit the bong. "She's fucking possessed with a freaky, little-kid-voiced Micheal Myers demon."

"Shit." Shane stood straight and stepped back. "And why'd you bring her here?"

The room was quiet for a moment other than Pink Floyd playing softly from the boombox.

"Well…" Phil started and faded.

"Because we trust you," Robin said. "We know you care about Holly and you'd want to help."

Shane blushed. "Yeah, I want to help. But I'm not an exorcist." He wandered to the right and sat on the couch, where he continued studying Holly. "She looks sick. I guess that makes sense for possessed people. I guess we have to figure out how it happened and—you think we need a priest?”

A high-pitched giggle came from the kitchen. Then it was coming from the bedroom. It sounded like it was at the front door, then settled on Holly.

“Fuck.” Shane leaned back on the couch as far as he could get from Holly.

“Told you,” Robin said, setting the bong on the table.

“You can’t save your friend,” Holly said in the child’s voice, only this time the tone vibrated the room as she spoke.

There was a presence behind it that made Phil shiver at her voice, and at that moment, he wanted to be anywhere else in the world other than in that room.

“You can’t even save yourselves,” Holly cackled. Her eyes went from Phil to Ryan to Robin to Shane. They pulsed, and thick blood seeped from the corners. It was dark and left a heavy trail behind it. “Moholam is coming. He will eat your souls, and we will take your flesh. And your own gluttony will be your downfall.”

Shane rose from his seat and slapped Holly across the face. “No! Bad demon!”

Robin covered her mouth. “What the fuck, Shane!”

He sank back to the couch. “Oh, yeah. The power of Christ compels you!” He rocked forward and slapped her again. “Get out of my friend, you asshole!”

Blood flooded from Holly’s mouth like a faucet. It ran, chunky, over her lips and drenched her front and then Shane’s chair. It ran over her legs and crawled across the floor, the dark crimson sludge seeming to take over the carpet an inch at a time.

“She’s mine!” Holly’s voice was no longer a child. It was gruff and deep. It was a demon that in no way could have walked the earth. It was evil in a way that sank into your thoughts and prodded.

Phil saw death in his mind. It was a vision of his mom and dad on their beds, bleeding from sliced throats. There was a vision of the town on fire as flames reached up into the dark sky with black smoke at their tips. His friends were ripped in half on the floor of the mall, with bloody entrails between them, and a bulging figure the likes of which he could not have imagined standing in the center of the food court beside that creepy custodian. The thing was easily twenty feet tall, with fiery tendrils flopping around its head. It had the face of a bull with fanged teeth and spiked arms. It was Moholam, loose in the world. He knew that.

"There's no stopping it," Phil muttered.

Ryan wept and cupped his bandaged arm. He was seeing it too. "No. That can't happen."

Robin clutched her chest.

"Fuck that!" Shane looked at the end table beside him, then the coffee table at his knees. He drew the drawer from the coffee table and grabbed two pipes from inside, a long wooden one, which would have been at home in the hands of a woodland wizard, and a short metal one that fit easily into any stoner's pocket. He held the wooden one vertically and pressed the metal one behind it, making a cross, and he shoved his ridiculous invention into Holly's face, screaming, "Cut it out, you fucking asshole!"

Phil's jaw dropped as the images left his mind.

Shane held the makeshift cross against Holly's forehead, and both the child's voice and the demonic one cried together.

Shane howled, "In the name of Christ, I said knock it the fuck off!"

The demons' voices faded, and Holly was out again. The room stank like blood, and all any of them heard for a solid minute was Pink Floyd and their own panting.

"Hell yeah." Shane sat back on the couch. He smiled at Robin. "What do we do now?"

Ryan walked over to Holly. He reached toward her face and stopped himself. "I don't know."

Phil came closer, and the smell of the strange blood registered. "You know what that smells like?"

Robin nodded. "It's in the sauce."

Shane picked up the bong. "I told you it was demons."

Phil shook his head. "You said it was aliens."

"Everyone knows aliens are really demons. They just hide their identity to fool the weirdos." He lit the bong and inhaled deeply.

"Fucking aliens." Ryan shook his head.

"We have to go back to the mall." Robin gazed at Holly with grief in her eyes. "We gotta figure out what's up with that maintenance man and this blood-sauce stuff. That has to be the key to getting that thing out of Holly."

Eleven

BENJAMIN HAD WAITED FOR night to fall and the mall to close. He had been patient, knowing one of his had been kidnapped—again—and it was almost time. It was okay, though. He knew it would sort itself out, and by the end of the night, his master would be pleased.

It was inevitable.

He dragged the body those kids had left in the hall until he stood in the center of the food court, then he pushed a few tables and chairs back so he had enough room. He placed the headdress over his head and pulled his knife from his belt.

Benjamin could smell his destiny in the air. There was a crisp, electric scent, blood and brimstone just on the other side, waiting to be released. It was like June 1976 all over again; only this time, it would work.

He plunged the blade into the dead kid's chest and scooped out a handful of cold, congealing blood. He wiped it on the hard floor, starting a circle around the body just above the head. He got a third of the way and had to return for more. He wiped the blood in streaks, connecting the strokes without a gap. He worked diligently, carefully, lovingly. This part mattered. This part had to be perfect. He had enough vessels and enough supplicants, but the ceremony had to be perfect.

With the circle done, he started on the star, The Star of Moholam, which was unknown to most. It would be a heptagram, a seven-pointed star in a mockery of the seven days, embracing the seven sins and containing a circle to hold his offering. It took five more trips for blood, but there was enough, and the circle was completed.

Benjamin sat in the middle. He balanced on the dead kid's chest and stroked the headdress's bony frame. He reached down, digging one hand inside the corpse's split face and the other hand inside the abdomen. He closed his eyes and began the chant.

From every corner of the food court, workers walked toward Benjamin. From Zen's Asian Delight walked three. The guys from Beer Battered Pretzel came, their swagger gone, only seriousness on their pale, hollow faces. Three came from The Boot. Two came from Quigly's. Stan and Chantal came from Jumbo Juice. Two more each came from Happy Burger, Suzuki Sushi, and Buffalo Chicken. They all surrounded The Star of Moholam, grabbed tables and chairs, and tossed them away, making room for the ceremony. Noise filled the mall as seats toppled and crashed into the counters of stores and gates. When they were done, they kneeled around the circle and waited.

Benjamin stopped chanting and pointed at one of the guys from the pretzel place. The guy stood. He was tall and blond, and as he moved toward the center of the star, he ripped his shirt from his body. When he reached Benjamin, he held out his hand, and the leader placed his blade there.

There was no thought or hesitation in what the pretzel guy did. He raised the blade to his throat as he leaned over Benjamin's headdress, and he sliced deep.

Blood gushed from his neck. It poured onto the center of the ceremonial headpiece, and he stood there, trembling. Stood there with his fists tight and arms bulging as he strained and kept himself upright as long as possible. As long as it took to do his task. Then he dropped to the floor, empty.

Benjamin pointed at Brad, the cashier from Quigly's. Brad stood and walked to the center as Satan's Fingers reached from between the headdress's bones and stretched. Brad picked the knife up from between the pretzel guy's fingers and opened his throat in a wide, bloody smile.

The chanting resumed from Benjamin and each of those surrounding him. Blood flowed into the headdress, and the cursed ceremonial garb soaked in each drop. It swelled as it filled itself. And as Brad toppled to the floor, Satan's fingers dripped crimson.

"What's going on in here?" a call came from the south, where the food court met the mall proper. It was Carl Stephens, the security officer who was supposed to be gone by that time of night. "What are all you people doing to him?"

Benjamin could not allow that man to ruin things. It had been too long coming, too much was at stake; it was his second attempt, and it had to go correctly. He might not have enough years to try a third time. He pointed at Carl, and the remaining two pretzel guys and the three Zen's Asian Delight workers leaped to their feet and ran.

"Oh, hell no." Carl turned and took off running. He was around the corner before Benjamin's acolytes were halfway there.

Benjamin didn't see what happened after that, but he knew.

Satan's fingers spread and stretched, and blood sprayed from them onto each of the remaining thirteen worshipers. They chanted together, and their eyes glowed yellow, with veins as red as their faces. They swelled within their skins and jumped to their feet and danced.

It was joyous. They moved as a group in a circle around the star, spinning and singing the words of the lost enlightened.

Gunshots were fired; Benjamin didn't count and didn't care.

Carl screamed from somewhere across the mall.

The lights above flashed and turned crimson. Blood sprayed, and the star vibrated on the ground. A minute later, only the Beer Battered

Pretzel employees limped back into the food court. They bled from their chests and dragged Carl from his legs. He moaned and left a trail of blood behind him.

Benjamin waved them closer, and the dancers parted to let them by.

They stood the security guard up. He struggled as they sliced a chasm in his throat and bled him dry into Benjamin's headdress. After they threw Carl out of the way, his killers joined the others in dance.

—

Robin puffed on her cigarette and tapped on the window as they drove across town. She and Ryan wore mostly clean, barely fitting clothes they had borrowed from Shane. Robin prayed they would be able to get into the mall. It was after hours, and none of them had even stopped to think of that. She didn't care, though. She would smash a window or break down a door or do whatever it took to get inside and find the answers. They had Holly now. They had to figure out how to save her.

Holly... Robin shook her head. How could she have let this happen? Not that she could protect her friend from everything in the world, but she had to believe she could have done something. It had been four days since she saw Holly. She could have helped had she known about it sooner, had she not ditched her friend for four days. Well, maybe not ditched, but she could have tried harder to find her.

"Uh, Robin?" Phil glanced in her direction as he drove. "I just remembered something I think you should know."

She didn't want to hear it, whatever it was. She sensed his hesitation, and on a night like that, it would be about something bad.

"What is it?" She sounded tired.

"You know, things have been so crazy today, and it slipped my mind—you know, with dealing with Holly and the fight and all."

"Just spit it out."

"Yeah. Well, when we were following you and Holly and Jud, I think I saw your mom. She was by Jumbo Juice, and she was walking away with a cup."

"No."

"I don't know what was in it—I can't prove it, but, you know, leaving Jumbo Juice, it could have been a smoothie."

"Fuck." Chills wrapped her arms, and her stomach churned sourly.

"It might not have been."

"Or she might have drank a big cup of that red blood shit."

"...Yeah."

She sighed. "Well, I guess we don't know. But we know Holly needs help. Let's figure out this Holly thing, and then I'll head home to check on her. Maybe if we figure out how to fix Holly, it'll fix her too."

"That makes sense."

"Fuck." How could she have let that happen? Her mom too? She knew there was something funny with that juice. Why didn't she warn Mom? Why didn't she do *something*?

She inhaled her smoke and tossed the butt. She pounded her fist on her lap. They had to fix it. They didn't have a choice.

Shane watched Holly from the couch, wishing he had taken mushrooms instead of acid. The way her eyes throbbed out of her skull and her aura flared like bright-red flames made him want to shudder. He could hear her teeth grinding, and even though the cross trick worked before, he wasn't sure it would again. There was something different now. Part of her aura seemed to flutter toward the door like something was calling it. And it was strong.

Either way, he had taped those pipes together, and they waited on the table in case he needed them.

"Let me out, Shane," she whined like a child. "I'm okay. I just had a bad day is all. Let me go."

He didn't answer. He had seen *The Exorcist* like a dozen times. He wasn't going to fall for that.

"Come on, Shane." She began lifting one leg and then the other while rotating her hips. The bloody sludge on her lap melted away, and she spread her legs as far as she could under her ropes. "I know I can do something for you. I know you've always wanted me."

She was right. He had always thought she was sexy. He would have been honored if she wanted him—most days. But not like this. He was more of a romantic at heart. He would have wanted to take her out and talk over dinner at the beach. He would have listened to her loves and dreams and pondered them with her. He would have wanted to connect, not just screw her on the couch in the living room—maybe that could have come after... but not like this.

Still she squirmed, moving her hips forward and up, back and down. Her pants seemed to tighten around her waist, exposing her curves in every region.

"Come on, Shane. You don't even have to untie me. Maybe just my feet so these pants can come off, and I can wrap my legs around you."

He shook his head no, but he could feel his pants getting tighter as well. He also saw something in her hair he didn't like. It wasn't solid, more of an ethereal growth, but he was sure horns were sprouting from the sides of her head. They curled up and forward. More raised from the rear, and they pointed at him. And he thought he saw blood dripping from their tips.

"This ain't right, man." He scooted away from her across the couch.

"Come on," she whined.

Her pants got darker. Blood spilled over from her waistline, soaking the chair. It ran from the bottoms of her pant legs, flowing over her shoes and pooling on the carpet stains from earlier.

"Oops," she giggled. "Don't mind that. It's just my time of the month. But we can still have fun. In other ways."

She opened her mouth in an O and curled her head forward and up. "I can make you so happy."

He shook his head and, reaching the end of the couch, nearly fell over the armrest.

She smiled, and her teeth grew into fangs. She snapped her mouth shut with a clap.

"What—" It was all Shane could say.

She giggled again, lowering her face toward her ropes.

"No."

She sank into the seat, lining up her mouth and the top strand of rope.

"No!" He reached for the cross. "Stop!"

There was one more giggle, and her mouth opened and closed over the rope. The sound was like slamming a book on a hard, wooden table, and the restraints flew backward as she lunged from her seat.

"Fuck!" Leaning over the table, he raised the cross.

She grabbed his hand and twisted it. There was a snap, and the cross clattered onto the table.

Shane didn't feel any pain right away. He saw the room shift to another realm as she grabbed him. The walls melted away, and skulls and fire and things with horns like hers danced. Blood covered it all. There was a roar in the distance, and his heart banged inside his chest like he had never felt before, not on any acid trip or, God forbid, coke high. He liked it mellow, and this was not that.

He screamed as the pain from his twisted wrist radiated up his arm.

He wished he could have cooked them all dinner before the whole mess started tonight. He thought that would have been a cool way to hang and laugh before his death came.

The demon's giggle pierced his eardrums, and he saw a thing where Holly's face had been. It was not her. It was the thing using her as a puppet. The demon, the alien, the monster behind the scenes. It stared into him, and he felt it rooting around inside his head.

She released his arm and grabbed his head with both hands. The demon laughed as she lifted him by his skull and slammed him into the wall.

Twelve

ROBIN GOT AN EERIE feeling as they parked outside the food court. It started as a tickle under her skin and a pull inside her belly that said *Go away*.

The lot was empty, and Phil stopped in what may have been the closest space.

As soon as he cut the engine and she opened the door, a wall of cold fell over her. It was a hot night, and the summer humidity fought the cold but it gained little ground. There was something ahead—something they were about to walk into—that was not just bad, but maybe the worst thing she had ever approached. She only wished she could explain it to Phil and Ryan; then she could convince them the whole thing was a bad idea.

But when she turned to them, she knew they felt it too.

"I don't know about this, guys." Ryan climbed out from the back seat. "Maybe we should come back tomorrow."

"Or call the police?" Phil wondered.

Robin imagined those options. Holly was at Shane's—possessed. How would she fare waiting overnight? She was like some sick ghost of herself, and what if the thing inside her was hurting her physically? Could they wait?

And calling the cops was tempting, but what would the cops do? How would she explain that her friend was possessed without them thinking she was crazy or on drugs? Drugs... they would use the entire thing as justification to bust Shane and not even help Holly. They might send her to the hospital, but they wouldn't go to the mall and investigate.

And what about Mom? If they didn't figure it out, Mom could be in just as much danger as Holly.

"No," Robin said. "We have to do this ourselves, and now. There's no other option."

"Shit." Ryan shook his head. "Okay."

"Alright." Phil gestured toward the door and started walking.

"Shit," Ryan repeated as he and Robin caught up.

The food court entrance was a glass wall at the peak of the U-shaped group of restaurants. Robin could see a reddish light inside, which didn't help her trepidation. The internal lights were usually whitish-yellow and bright, and though she didn't think she had ever been there after hours to compare, what she saw in there did not look right, even if the usual lighting was turned off.

They paused at the door, each looking in, each hoping the others would call off the foolish endeavor before it went any farther. Through the glass, Robin could see chairs and tables scattered about. It was like a hurricane had gone through and tossed everything aside. Then she saw something over the mess, arms in the air. Something was happening in there.

She grabbed the door, and the others stared at her. She put a finger over her lips, *Shhh*, and pulled.

It opened. She was surprised it wasn't locked. She figured the security guy just hadn't been by for some reason, but she had little time to question it as the chanting struck her. It was loud. All the voices together vibrated her chest. She couldn't see what they were doing, but the repeated words and the flickering light told her she wanted no part of it. They filled her mind with feelings of dread as she crouched and snuck up to the wall of discarded furniture. They made her think of pain and sadness. The sounds made her want to hurt herself.

She clenched her fists as she reached a sideways table and peeked over the top. She felt Phil and Ryan on either side of her, raising their heads.

What she saw was like a punch in the gut. She wanted to cry, and she wanted to puke. The was blood everywhere. She could see glimpses of bodies on the floor through the dancing chanters. Who they were and if they were alive or dead was another question—the first one being: were she and her friends going to live through this?

Ryan sank, whispering, "Fuck, fuck, fuck."

She wished she had looked away too. There came a gap in the chanters, and she saw the center of the crowd. It was the maintenance man, or something resembling him. His face was his, but only partly. It was a demon, like Holly. It was moving under his skin like it was fighting to get out. And the blood. So much blood flew from its headpiece.

The gap filled in with revelers, and Robin realized she could move again. She dropped down, and Phil followed her.

"What do we do?" Ryan hissed.

"Cops," Phil whispered. "We definitely need cops."

He was right.

"There's a payphone by the bathrooms," Robin said. She could barely hear herself; she hoped they could.

"Payphone," Phil repeated.

"Come on." Robin crawled. She had to stay low; her fear wouldn't have it any other way. She went toward the exit and turned left, stopping at the door into the back halls beside Happy Burger. She waited for her friends, and she pushed it open as quietly as she could.

The bar went in slowly, so slowly.

Robin's heart slammed into her chest. She couldn't imagine what would happen if they were caught; she wouldn't let herself think that way. She only knew it would be bad and it would be bloody.

The bar made a soft clunk as it triggered the lock, and the door opened.

She held the door tight in her hand and went through. She held it for Ryan and Phil. She couldn't risk letting go or even think of one of them being too loud with it.

They slipped through, and she gently let it close, fearing the clunk of the latch. She was going to have a heart attack if it was loud. She closed her eyes as steel met steel with the faintest of noises.

She stood, regaining her breath. "This way."

Ryan followed Robin and Phil into the back hallway, and his stomach cramped in on itself. He knew he was going to throw up at any moment; there was no way around it. The whole situation was going from bad to worse, and what he really wanted to do was just run away. Run far away from it all.

But what would his friends think of him if he did that?

He had known Phil since kindergarten, Robin soon after that. They should have known this was too much. The blood, what were obviously dead bodies, they should have turned right around and left.

They ran past pipes and wires and dark crevices in the walls. They ran past the entrances to stores, and it dawned on Ryan who those people were. They weren't just random guys and girls in the middle of the food court; those were other restaurant employees. Those were people who had been beside him, served the red sauce, and as he passed the next business entrances, he understood there could be more of them just behind those doors.

There was nowhere safe in the food court. Not the halls or the shops or anywhere. They were running to another hall with a phone, but that wasn't going to be any safer. They needed to turn around and leave, or—

There was a slam from behind them. A door had crashed shut, and the echo ran up the hallway and made Ryan's heart leap into his throat.

"Guys," he whispered over his heaving breaths. "Did you hear that?"

Phil turned as they ran. "What was that?"

"I don't know." But he did know. "Someone's following us."

"Come on," Robin hissed. They had to be halfway there. She moved faster, and so did they.

But that sound! It had to have been a door. It had to have been someone following them, right?

As quiet as they were trying to be, their feet slapped the concrete floor as they ran. It echoed, and even though Ryan had no proof, he was sure some of the echoes he heard were coming from behind him—others' feet.

"Guys," he hissed.

Phil shushed him.

Ryan looked behind them. He didn't see anyone, but he knew they were back there. *Someone* was back there.

"Yes," Robin whispered as she reached the door to the court. She grabbed the handle and pulled, and Phil took the opening edge in his hand and helped. She slipped through. He was right behind her, holding it open for Ryan.

Ryan moved faster, praying. His friends had made it through, but he still heard the echoes. There was still someone in the hallway, and they were getting closer.

He took a step through the opening, and something stopped him from moving forward. It was hard on his shoulder. Then he realized there was pain there too.

Ryan looked down. There was a blade in him, stabbing into his shoulder and pulling him backward.

"No!" It left his mouth as a scream. He knew he was supposed to be quiet, but he needed his friends. "Help!"

He saw Phil's wide eyes as he was yanked backward and the door slammed shut.

Robin's eyes were on the payphone. It was just beyond the restroom doors. Then Ryan screamed.

She wanted to go back and slap him. What the hell was wrong with him? Didn't he realize they had to be quiet?

It took a second longer for her brain to process the word *Help*. She spun in time to see the door slam shut and watch Phil grab at the push bar, trying to follow. But the bar wouldn't push, and the door wouldn't open.

Ryan was gone, and they were trapped in the tiny hallway with nothing but the bathrooms and the phone, and as she looked out into the food court, she realized the chanting had diminished. It was still there but quieter, with fewer voices behind it. She couldn't see the center, only a wall of discarded chairs and tables, but she knew what it meant: they had heard the noise, and they were coming.

The phones—the phones were the only option.

She ran past the bathroom doors and grabbed the first receiver. She raised it to her ear as her fingers hovered, poised over the keypad. She waited for the click and the dial tone. They didn't come.

Fuck. Was it broken?

Robin dropped it and moved to the next one. Her ear against the phone, she waited.

Nothing. Were they all broken?

She hung it up and lifted it again. Still nothing.

"Robin," Phil called her from behind. "Come on."

She ignored him. There was one more phone. That one had to work. She lifted the receiver and put it to her head. She held it there and looked into the court. Eight people were coming toward her.

She saw Stan, her manager, and dear god, he looked like Holly. Waxy skin, yellow eyes, a strange, blank expression on his face.

They were all possessed.

She shook her head, and the receiver slipped from her grip. "No!"

They were reaching for her.

"Robin!"

She turned and saw Phil. He was pounding on the men's room door, and it wasn't opening.

They grabbed her by the wrist, and she screamed.

Phil ran over and tried to pry the hands from her, and others grabbed him.

They both howled as they were dragged into the food court.

Thirteen

WHEN SHANE OPENED HIS eyes, he saw only blackness. Then he saw stars, and the stars danced to the sound of a repeated thrum. They streaked in front of his face, melted, dove, and launched into the air. They formed planets and galaxies, and he saw a Big Bang. It was nice. But he thought there should have been music.

While what he saw might have been a shock to a lot of people, Shane knew immediately he was tripping and the things before him were not real. They made him smile, and he knew he had to figure out what was going on, but if there was one thing he had learned from a thousand journeys into the psychedelic world, it was that panicking never helped. He was like the turtle in that old fable. He would get to where he needed to be, but only by taking his time and getting it right.

He reached for the closest planet, and while he would have expected to see his hand go right through it, he saw nothing. He did, however, feel something. It was hard and metallic. It had ridges and structure. He followed it up and around, and suddenly, the blackness, the droning hum around him, and the earthy scents and humidity all made sense. He was in a trunk.

He wondered if it was his trunk. His trunk was pretty big. He had two people in it with lots of room when he went with friends to the drive-in in Estero last year.

If it was his trunk, it meant two things: (1) there was no way out until someone opened it, and (2) he was pretty sure he knew what else was in there.

The car slowed and turned. A series of thumps.

He waited. That was all he could do right now. He felt a rising pain in his left wrist and vaguely remembered Holly knocking something from his hand. He wasn't going to focus on that, though.

He would get to where he needed to be. Hopefully he could help Holly when they got there.

Robin immediately recognized the feeling behind her as they threw her in the center of the chanting mall workers. She was on top of someone.

She turned from the mob of employees and sensed the slick wetness. She smelled the blood, and then she saw dead men below her.

"Fuck!" She spun, but they had tied her arms and legs. She squirmed to get out of the pile and pushed into Phil, beside her.

"What the hell?" Phil shouted. He was tied too. "Let us go!"

She tried rolling into the crowd, and one of them kicked her back toward the middle. It was Chantal.

"Chantal?" she cried. "Help us!" But Chantal's eyes told the truth. Her new friend was just as possessed as Holly, and it made Robin's heart ache. Those eyes, that skin—no one deserved that, definitely not her friends.

Robin took in each face in the crowd. Every one of them was a young food court employee. They were from the pretzel place, the sub shop, the pizza place—all of them. They were manic and overcome with frenzy, and she was sad for them all.

Blood sprayed from the maintenance man's flailing headdress onto Robin's face, and she spit out a glob that got into her mouth. It was rancid. It tasted sour and oily, and she knew instantly that was what had been in the secret sauce bottle. It was the source of all of this.

Streams of it rained on her, and she turned to the center of the circle. The worst part of all it was waiting there, and though she had seen the tentacles and the leader in glances, she didn't want to take in the entirety of it. She was scared to see the evil that could do that to those people, could kill the people she was lying on, could control the malevolence there, but she had to.

His face, God his face was repulsive. She could tell it was the custodian, but but it was more. His skin was his. His skull below the movement was too. But there was something trying to make his face into its. It bulged under the nose and cheeks. It stretched outward around the temples and forehead. It was like a wide mask of a face was being inflated under the skin, and Robin had a feeling that when it was done inflating, that thing was going to be what was real and not the custodian.

Blood splashed her in the eyes. That damn headpiece kept spraying everyone like a Willy Water Bug, the weird lawn toy she had when she was a kid that sprayed hose water all over the yard. Blood coated everything within twenty feet, and sensations of anger and sadness drilled into her.

She watched them chant, and she knew there was only sadness left in the world. The only way to cure it was to join the chant. The way to free herself was to be one of them and let the anger take hold. She could hack and slash. She could make more blood for the headdress, for the master. That was what was right. It would please him, and it would please her.

No, it wasn't right. They were there to find a cure, to help Holly, and—maybe Holly didn't need help. Maybe Holly needed to bring blood. Maybe she needed to dance and chant with Holly in Moholam's grace.

Robin felt her lips move. She didn't know why at first, then she felt it. They wanted to say the words. They were parched and wanted to drink the master's blood.

Something shoved her, and she turned. It was Ryan, bleeding from the shoulder with terror in his eyes.

She felt a hum from her other side. Phil was chanting. He was saying the words oh so softly, but she could feel it, and it made her want to open her mouth wide and scream them for the master.

Two things happened next, and Robin was too intoxicated by the blood and song to know which happened first. There was something crawling on her foot. She had known a kid in middle school who owned a Burmese python, and he was always asking everyone if they wanted to hold it. When she did, the thing walked over her skin and climbed her arm with a strange pressure that she could never describe and would never forget. The way it flexed and squeezed to keep its balance as it moved, the pressure of its muscles over hers as it pushed itself onward—it was creepy, not just because of the way it moved, but because she knew the thing was using her and if it was large enough, it would stretch its mouth wide and swallow her whole. That feeling was back, and it was crawling up her leg. It was swaying and pressing and slithering over her thigh. It was on its way toward her face.

It was when Phil shouted, "What's on my leg?" that she noticed the other thing happening.

From the food court entrance, the same one she had come through, someone new joined them. There was a split second when she hoped it was someone who could help, but as the chanters split and she saw who it was, every grain of hope vanished.

It was not help. It was Holly. She was dragging Shane along the floor like he was nothing but an empty sack.

Behind them, with yellowed eyes and a zombie-like walk, was Robin's mother.

"Holly, help!" Ryan screamed. He could see it in her face. She wasn't going to help, but he had to try. Maybe he could break through to her. "Please, Holly! We love you!"

"Holly," Phil moaned.

Holly dropped Shane at the outer edge of the circle. He lay there with such stillness that Ryan wasn't sure if he was passed out or dead.

"Holly, please!" Ryan begged.

She set her eyes on him and came closer. His heart quickened. She was going to help him. He had gotten through to her. She walked past Robin and Phil and stood at his feet.

"That's it. Untie me."

But she didn't. She turned to the gap she had entered through and watched Robin's mom walk to the center. The woman looked confused, but she kept coming, and the crowd closed in behind her. They chanted louder, and the waving tendrils on the custodian's headpiece soaked her with crimson poison.

"Mom, run!" Robin screamed. She squirmed but didn't get anywhere. Whatever snake-like thing was crawling up her body continued up her hips. "Please, Mom, get out of here!"

Holly took Robin's mom by the hand and guided her over her daughter and Phil. Holly led her until she was standing directly next to the custodian.

The leader sat on a body in the middle of the circle, looking oblivious to anything other than his chanting. He didn't even acknowledge the horrific malformations of his face as his skin stretched and pressed into unnatural shapes.

Ryan couldn't hear well under the repetitious drone of the group, but he thought he heard a child say, "Good," just before Holly pulled a kitchen knife from her pocket and slowly sank it into Robin's mother's throat.

Robin screamed.

Even under the echoing chant, it broke through and pained Ryan's ears.

"Mom!"

Her mother did not answer. The knife flicked outward in a forward stroke, and her neck burst almost in half. Her blood shot from the gap, drenching the maintenance man's headdress and face.

Robin screamed again.

That one wasn't just painful to Ryan. He could hear Robin's heart breaking as her mother stood over the center of the circle, holding herself as firm as a statue while blood sprayed and bubbled over the mastermind of this insanity.

"Please! Oh my god!"

"Holly, stop!" Phil howled.

The lights in the room glowed a brighter red. The bloody shapes on the floor wiggled and squirmed underneath Ryan, his friends, and the growing pile of bodies. The chanting grew louder, and Robin's mom thumped to the floor beside the others.

"Jesus!" Ryan wiggled, trying to slip away. His shoulder screamed in pain as he mistakenly used it. Then, Holly reached down and took him by his good arm, guiding him to his feet. "Please, no."

She didn't answer. The child's voice inside her giggled.

"Please, Holly! No."

"Holly, no!" Phil shouted.

Robin sobbed. She closed her eyes and shuddered. The thing crawled onto her belly.

"I'm your friend, Holly," Ryan pleaded. "Don't do this!"

Ryan trembled. His legs wobbled like they were made of nothing but flimsy paper. He stared into the custodian's headdress. The tendrils sprayed blood into his face as they waved hypnotically. He found himself unable to look away as the floor shook beneath his feet.

It was so clear as he studied the bones that made up the headpiece, the moving Fingers of Satan, and the blood flying everywhere. He was a part of something bigger now. He was going to help usher in the new children, the ones who would take the Earth to its next plane of existence. He didn't matter. His blood mattered. His blood was a key that would make it all possible.

He stood upright and rigid. He would give every last drop. No matter what else happened, he would give it all.

Fourteen

S HANE WATCHED THROUGH SLITTED eyes as what used to be his friend sliced into a woman's neck. He saw the horns glisten in the room's red light and a flicker of fire in her eyes as the blood poured from the woman's neck onto the monster in the center.

Yes, he knew it was a monster. He could see it through the lumpy skin on its face. It may have been hiding inside a person, but that person was gone now. The only thing inside that fleshy vessel was a beast waiting to claw its way out once it was strong enough.

Some may have called what they were seeing a scene of death, but Shane knew better; to that thing, it was a birth.

Holly picked up Ryan and maneuvered him into position.

Shane was running out of time. He had been playing possum since Holly opened the trunk and he saw where he was. It was the only way to help his friends. But now, it was time to act. If he didn't, that thing was going to pop out of the man in the center like a stripper through a fleshy, oversized cake, and his friends would all be doomed.

Holly reached for her knife, and Shane knew it was now or never.

He sprang up and snagged the doughy snake thing on Robin's leg and tossed it over the crowd. The red light and waving hands of dancers were shooting stars across his vision. The walls melted, and faces showed their true selves as LSD pulsed through his brain.

Horns. There were horns everywhere.

Another pace, and he grabbed the creature on top of Phil. Through a barrage of pain in his wrist, he threw it away. He spread his arms wide as he took the next step and slammed into Holly mid-waist.

He hated doing it. Inside, behind the evil thing controlling her, was his friend. But the horns said it all. The beast was in charge, and he had to treat her as an enemy.

Shane felt the breath leave her chest. He saw the knife drop from her grip as he drove her backward and into the crowd. Hands grabbed hold of her. He felt them grasp at his arms and body, and he pulled back, letting Holly and six others tumble down. He saw the faces of those demonic dancers, their eyes huge and bulging, their smiles crooked and too big for their heads. He wanted to think it was the drugs, but he knew what he was seeing was real. It was the things inside them waiting to be birthed a new.

He glanced at his friends to prepare his next move, and chills ran through his body.

In the middle of the widening red aura, in the cloud of anger and sorrow where those blood-spraying tendrils flicked and whipped, Ryan had picked Holly's knife up from the floor. His head had sprouted the buds of horns. His eyes were plumping to the size of plums. His smile—it was monstrous. Ryan turned the blade in his taped hands, and he carved a chasm from one side of his neck to the other.

"No!" Shane howled.

Blood spurted onto the leader and his tentacled hat, and the face that had been fighting to consume its human settled into place.

There was a loud scream as the circle and the seven-pointed star on the floor lit up like they were made of neon. The room rocked. The ceiling creaked, and dust and plaster rained down. The chanters sang even louder.

Shane could hear them trying to force themselves into his head. They were trying to claw into his thoughts the way they must have done to Ryan—Ryan, who swayed forward and back as his blood sprayed weaker and weaker and his large eyes rolled back into his head.

Images from the worst moments in Shane's life flipped through his mind like some kind of slide show. His parents scolding him. His teachers telling him he would never be anything more than a bum. His hands in his suit pockets as he stared out over Carrie's coffin while they lowered it into her grave. His mom and dad had told him he didn't have to wait for it, but he had to see. He needed to know his baby sister was there, in her final resting place, before he could move on.

He saw himself lighting up for the first time, drinking anything he could get his hands on, and swallowing pill after pill to numb the pain. But there was one scene that whatever this force was showing him didn't want to come through, a scene he fell back to every day. And he would not let that one go, no matter how hard they pushed.

It was two years ago, after a long solo date with mushrooms, paper, and a tail of X. He sat on his couch, facing the morning traffic as it passed by, with the sun rising and his .357 revolver in his hand. The gun was rising slowly toward his temple because that day, even the chemicals couldn't hold back the sea of worthlessness he felt for himself. It was time to pull the trigger and be done.

Until he saw her.

Her face was in the window. She was smiling. She couldn't stop the tears from running down his cheeks, but she could make sure he heard her, and he did.

That was why he was here today. That was why he stood and walked forward through the shower of blood and the chanting and the daggers stabbing at his mind, trying their hardest to penetrate. He wouldn't let them in. He'd had a million things try to sour his trips before. He'd had the practice. They would not get in. He was here for his friends. He was here to spread love. He was here to say no to these assholes and do what he came to do.

From the back of his pants, Shane pulled the cross-shaped tire iron he had smuggled in from his trunk. He held it ahead as he pulled the knife from Ryan's hand and dropped it into Phil's. Phil cut at his ropes as Shane gently guided Ryan to the floor.

The whole building was shaking and howling like an oncoming train, and Shane put the smile back on his face. That was where it belonged. He looked past the thing breaking through the custodian's facade, ripping his skin into bloody shreds as it emerged, and he saw her. She was a white light just beyond the circle, watching him and loving him. She was waiting for him.

Shane wound back the tire iron and swung with everything he had. "The power of Christ compels!" he screamed as his steal smashed into bone.

The headdress squealed as bone cracked and broke free. Fragments sailed into the air, and a tendril grabbed Shane's wrist.

"Fuck you!" he screamed, and pulled back the iron. He brought it straight down, and a dozen shards of bone went flying. Two tendrils slipped out and flopped on the floor like dying worms.

"Power of Christ, motherfucker!" He brought it down again.

The headdress shifted to the left, and the thing inside the custodian opened its fanged mouth. It screamed, in pain, and as Shane raised his weapon once more, the custodian's hand shot upward, driving a blade into the dead center of Shane's chest.

Shane's smile never left his face, even as he took his last breath.

Phil cut his hands and feet free just in time to watch Shane fall. The chanting was quieter, and the probing into his head was weaker as he stood and put the knife in Robin's hand. But the building was still shaking, and the blood was still spraying. It wasn't over yet, and it wouldn't be if he didn't find a way to keep up Shane's work.

He spun and grabbed the tire iron from Shane's hand. He wanted to weep as he saw the blood and the content smile on Shane's face, but there would be time for that later.

His fellow mall employees took a step toward him, and he raised the steel cross between them. They froze, and he looked into their bulging eyes. They wanted to take him down. Their massive grins showed grinding teeth full of eagerness. But the cross was somehow holding them back.

He turned and swung, bashing the maintenance man's headdress as hard as he could. Bone went flying, and the headpiece hung from the side of the leader's head.

"Phil!" It was Holly in her own voice. "Stop, Phil! You have to stop!" She looked completely normal, like the demon had left her. But it couldn't have been real. It was a ploy.

He turned back toward the center of the circle, and the thing that had been the custodian was climbing to its feet. Weirdly, it was larger than the man had been. Its coveralls were bursting at the seams, and its arms stretched from the ends of its sleeves. Its ankles were several inches below its cuffs. It had grown, and not just a little. And its face—that was something that would haunt Phil as long as his heart beat.

It was looking at Phil, and it swung the custodian's blade toward him so fast it was almost a blur.

Phil jumped backward. He raised and turned the iron. There was a clang as steel met steel.

Phil sensed his good luck escaping. The thing was massive, and as it stood, it raised Phil's target. In a few seconds, it was going to be impossible to reach that headdress, especially if he had to aim past the monster's huge arms. He had to end this now.

He swung as hard as he could at the headpiece. There was a cracking sound both from the bony artifact and the ceiling above. The ground leaped up, and Phil felt himself thrown forward.

The monster screamed and fell backward as the headpiece slipped off, crumbling apart, and Phil thudded against him. They hit the ground together, and a chunk of concrete burst through the ceiling and crashed on top of one of the demon's minions. Blood sprayed, and another, even bigger piece flattened the two from the pretzel shop.

Phil pushed himself up and realized he was straddling the stone-faced demon's chest. The problem was the tire iron was no longer in his hand. All he had was his fists, so he used them.

Phil punched the demon in the face over and over. Its rock-hard bones hurt his hands, but he did it again and again.

Robin showed up at his side and kicked the demon in the head.

The ceiling fell in, one chunk of concrete after another. It crashed through the roofs of Zen and The Boot. It destroyed the counter at Quigly's and crushed four more chanting workers into piles of gore. The floor under Phil ripped open with a two-inch-wide crack, splitting the bloody sigil in two.

Blood leaked from the demon's mouth, while on the ground, the headdress lay still. Its tentacles were dormant and shriveling.

Mall employees stared at each other as their eyes shrank back into their heads and their smiles slimmed. They grew silent, marveling at the blood and collapsing mall as if waking from a dream. Another hunk of ceiling leveled a Boot worker, and the rest turned. They ran toward the exit, dodging ceiling tiles and concrete chunks.

Phil started to smile. It was working. Then his midsection was set on fire. Pain seized him as his fist swung down, and he looked. A knife was in his belly, and the demon was pushing it higher. It was tearing through his stomach like nothing, and all he could think was that his guts were about to spill out across the floor and he didn't want to lose any of them.

He tried to scream, but his lungs were tight and wouldn't move. He grabbed the thing's hand as it pushed. The best he could do was hold on as it rose up his belly a quarter inch at a time.

He was going to die there. All he had wanted was to save some money to go to a music festival, and there he was fighting a goddamn demon. This wasn't worth $4.50 an hour.

His lungs filled with just enough air for him to scream, and Holly walked over and stood behind the demon's head.

Other than the blood coating her face, she looked sane. She looked like Holly again, and she held the tire iron in both hands, raising it up over her head.

At that moment, something happened to the demon. His body withered. His face shrunk. His skin didn't quite match his old one—it hung a bit saggy—but the man inside was clearly visible as the mall custodian again, not whatever the hell was filling him like an overstretched balloon. He held up his hand toward Holly, and he opened his mouth to speak.

"Wait." He released the blade in Phil's gut, and Phil toppled to the side.

Robin held back her foot, but she was poised to kick again. The man opened his hand in an offering gesture to Holly. "I'm... I'm your real father."

There was a silence between them all as rocks crashed down, wood cracked, and neon signs exploded. The rumble in the floor had stopped, but the air was just as turbulent with doubt.

Holly's teeth clamped together, and her fists tightened. She brought the tire iron down, and it collided with Benjamin Hawthorne's skull. His face crumpled in like a piece of rotten fruit. He gasped, and she raised the tool and brought it back down. His forehead smashed inward, and this time, the blood spraying was his own.

She slammed it down three more times, until Robin took her by the shoulder and stopped her, and there was nothing left of the man's face but a bloody pile of flesh and bone.

"Fuck you, Dad!" Holly tossed the tire iron to the side.

Fifteen

ROBIN SAT BESIDE PHIL'S hospital bed as the monitors gently beeped and Jerry Springer interviewed a woman who didn't know which of three men was the father to her baby boy. The crowd was booing the woman when Phil opened his eyes and, after searching the room, smiled at her before wincing in pain.

Phil was going to live; at least, that's what the doctors said. They had to remove four feet of his small intestine, and the recovery was going to be long, likely making him miss Lollapalooza, but Robin had her fingers crossed that they could still do it, though possibly a later show. They needed it after the start of the summer they had.

She held his hand, and he smiled, and they watched the show until he inevitably drifted off again.

Robin had escaped the ordeal at the mall with little more than a few scratches. It was a miracle that she and Holly were able to drag Phil out of the food court without a chunk of concrete killing them; even more of a miracle was that the police showed up just as they reached the parking lot, with an ambulance following shortly after.

It turned out that a Taco Dave's employee saw the flashing lights and the roof collapsing from across the street and called the cops. When Robin and Phil found that out, they vowed they would forever be loyal customers.

Once Phil was on the way to the hospital in the ambulance, Robin found the cops unimpressed with Robin's or Holly's or any other mall employees' stories about what had happened in there. They understood it was some kind of satanic ritual driven by the grumpy old maintenance guy, but none of the rest of it made sense to them. They didn't have a section on possession or demonic earthquakes in their manuals. With so much blood, they had to assume it was all a mind-control, cult-type scenario. With that, they arrested everyone until they sorted some of it out, and the parents, some of whom had significant local political persuasion, put pressure on the mayor's office.

In the end, all the minors were released except Holly, who had no explanation for how her parents were found nearly decapitated in her kitchen.

Some of the pretzel guys' families were found the same way, but since they were dead under the rubble, they couldn't be charged.

The police just couldn't let Holly's parents' murders go, even if they didn't know how to explain the motive other than a kid caught up in a cult.

Robin and Phil were worried Holly was going to get the blame for everything—*Maintenance Man and Estranged Love Child Drive Cult Murders* was a headline she expected to appear in the newspaper any day now. Robin loved Holly, and she knew she was possessed for all the bad stuff, but it still made her queasy, regardless of the facts. She didn't want to see Holly go to prison—even if she couldn't get those images out of her head.

Phil woke and fell asleep again before Springer was over.

Robin flipped through the channels. She passed one with a mother cooking dinner, and her tears started up again. She missed Mom. She missed her so much. She was hardly able to stand at the funeral, and her dad was a silent mess. All she could do was hate herself for every hurtful thought and word she had ever had and hoped to God that Mom was looking down from Heaven with forgiveness. She wished she could have had one more day, one more night in the kitchen helping Mom cook dinner and laughing the way they did before she was in high school and all she did in her free time was hang out with friends. It was something she didn't think she would ever forgive herself for, no matter how much she knew it was just part of growing up.

The single funeral home in Golden Palms was full to capacity that week, but the only other service Robin could force herself to go to was Shane's.

Despite his differences with his parents, they stood there together and wept through it all. It was likely the biggest funeral the town had seen in years. Regardless of Shane's reputation among police, the love of his friends packed the room in a way Robin was not expecting. It filled her with such heartfelt appreciation that she had been among his friends that she doubted she was even worthy. He was laid to rest beside his sister, Carrie.

Robin would always remember his smile.

Ryan's family didn't offer a service, at least not a public one. Robin thought his parents blamed his friends for his job and his love of music, both of which led to his death in their minds. It hurt Robin's heart that she couldn't say goodbye, but she and Phil both promised they would find a way to pay their respects in their own ways.

She flipped the channels and found *Star Trek IV* playing on HBO. Mom had liked that one, so she left it there and remembered Mom's laugh as Kirk shouted, "A double dumbass on you!" It made her smile and cry at the same time.

She turned to Phil. That poor bastard had been through Hell and back since school got out, and she knew half of it was because of her, because he had a crush on her. At the beginning of the summer, she would have said he didn't have a chance—that he was too meek—but the horrible events had changed her mind, even if it took her a little time to see it. He had risked his life. He had fought that demon, and together, they had lived. She had always had love for him as a friend, but she couldn't deny there was more than that there after everything. Thinking about where it might go gave her a warm feeling.

She would make sure they made it to a Lollapalooza. They would celebrate with Ryan and Shane in their hearts, and they were going to have a blast.

***

Holly sat in a Golden Palms Police Station solitary-confinement holding cell. It seemed like she hadn't stopped crying in the week since she had been there. She knew she didn't have control, and she only somewhat remembered her parents' deaths, but she still blamed herself. She could have gotten a job somewhere else. She could have fought harder against whatever was inside her. She just knew there was something more she should have been able to do to stop it.

The others that had been possessed came and went. She knew, like her, they remembered more than they admitted to. None of them looked each other in the eyes. None of them said much of anything at all.

Lawyers and cops streamed in and out. There were arguments, apparently, about whether she was going to be tried as a minor or an adult and whether she should be sent to the adult county jail or the juvenile jail until trial. When the tears came, she didn't care which. She only knew she wanted out of that tiny little space where she couldn't even tell if it was day or night except for the hour she got to spend in the enclosed basketball court every afternoon.

Not that she played basketball. She didn't play anything. She spent that hour every day with her back to the wall, sitting and wondering if there was going to be any kind of future for her—and if she deserved one.

Metal rattled and clanged outside her door, and it swung open. It felt a little early for her yard time, but she was happy to have it. She rose from the floor, expecting to see Officer Wilson, her usual bridge to the outside world, but instead of the curly-headed corrections officer, she found herself face-to-face with a tall, dark-haired policeman. He lifted his sunglasses, and Holly did a double take.

His eyes were yellow, with red veins crisscrossing their surfaces. He grinned, and Holly could smell the yeasty scent of bloodied pretzel dough on his breath.

A high-pitched giggle escaped her lips.

Acknowledgements

Food Court of the Damned was a lot of work, through long nights and weekends. It would not exist without the effort and kindness of many people. I thank you all and regret those I may have missed. This is just a token.

Christina Hitz — Thank you for sacrificing time together, encouraging me, and picking up all the pieces I missed through my absent-mindedness. Thank you for encouraging me and being there when I needed you.

My Editor: **Heather Ann Larson**, your keen eyes and attention to detail really helped to pull this book together. Thank you.

My Cover Artist: **Matt Seff Barnes**, this beautiful cover was an inspiration. Like all your work, it is amazing. Thank you.

My Patreon members: Thank you for your support along this journey. It was a blast writing as you read. Special thanks to **Jay Bower** and **Jordan Triplett**.

About the Author

D.W. Hitz loves the outdoors and enjoys making it a background character in his work. He devours stories in all mediums. He enjoys writing in the genres of Horror, Supernatural/Paranormal Thriller, and Science Fiction/Fantasy. He aspires to tell stories that thrill the heart and stimulate the imagination.

When not writing, D.W. enjoys spending time with his family, hiking, camping, and playing with the dogs.

———

Stay up to date with D.W. by becoming a member at
patreon.com/dwhitz

What's Next?

Check out more horror by D.W. Hitz and Fedowar Press.

Garrets Lodge by D.W. Hitz

Something is stirring in the woods outside Custer Falls. A haunted place that's been waiting a very long time.

Wanda heads out on a hike with friends. Stevie and Honey flee into the woods from the cops. They all think the woods will be their salvation until they find the terrors at Garrets Lodge.

Our Trip Through Hell by D.W. Hitz

Missy was always forbidden from visiting the abandoned cemetery. She listened for most of her life, but now her father's tales of buried gold and family treasure are proving too tempting for her and her friends to resist.

On a cold November night, it becomes a portal to Hell. If they want to return, they'll have to fight for it.

Camp Slasher Lake: Volume 3

A tribute to the glorious slasher movies of the 1980s, Volume 3.

Featuring stories by Jonathan Maberry, Will Suffer, MJ Mars, Brian G. Berry, Megan Stockton, Jay Bower, Eric Butler, M Ennenbach, RJ Roles, Angel Van Atta, and D.W. Hitz

Uncanny Valley Days by C.J. Sampera

Rocked by grief and recurring apparitions of her dead brother, Olivia is losing her grip on reality and may have inadvertently invoked a cybernetic, serial-killing slasher demon. Or is it all in her head?

Bloodtooth by D.W. Hitz

After nightmares begin in the small town of Custer Falls, Montana, in 1992, it'll be thirty years before they end.

After Wes Henson and his friends' field trip to Bloodtooth Caverns, everything changes. All they did was stray off the path. They didn't expect to break their bones and discover an ancient relic. But once it's in Wes's hands, he's the one that has to put it back. Because when this evil is awake, no one's dreams are safe.

Thank You for Reading